CHRISTMAS IN LYREBIRD LAKE

Where Christmas miracles can *happen…*

For midwives Tara and Maeve, the sleepy town of Lyrebird Lake is the haven they've always wanted. So they're determined to make their first Christmas there special!

Neither of them are looking for love— but this year, with the help of some Lyrebird Christmas magic, the celebrations will be beyond their wildest imaginings…

You won't want to miss this fabulous new festive duet from Fiona McArthur:

MIDWIFE'S CHRISTMAS PROPOSAL

&

MIDWIFE'S MISTLETOE BABY

Dear Reader

Welcome to Rayne and Maeve in Lyrebird Lake at Christmas time.

Wow. I hope you have fun with this. I was grinning all the way through. Rayne and Maeve wrote their story and I was just trying to keep up with them—two people with *sooo* much sexual chemistry between them, and both of them such determined people in their own right, with really tough dilemmas.

Most of my heroes and heroines are pretty private, and they prefer it if I leave the bedroom door firmly closed—but, while still avoiding anatomical explanations, Rayne and Maeve are so aware of the physical in each other they just can't keep their hands off and sometimes forget to shut the door. But it's still sweet.

So it's not surprising that after an explosive first night, right at the beginning, Maeve falls pregnant. As Rayne says, 'If there was one night when, no matter how many precautions were used, a determined sperm would get through, *that* was the night.'

Fast forward nine months and Rayne returns, unaware that Maeve is about to have his baby—and as a guy emotionally scarred by his childhood and with no male role model, he can't see how he can become the kind of father Maeve's baby deserves.

Maeve has to come to terms with the fact that Rayne walked away, didn't answer her letters, and let her down in her pregnancy. But he's here now—exactly what she so desperately wanted for Christmas—and after the first day with him back she believes in him…believes that Rayne has the potential to share the love he's never had a chance to share. She just has to help him to see it, and hopefully he'll become a believer before she has this baby. Thankfully she's in Lyrebird Lake, and with all the people she needs around her, this is the place to do it.

I'd really love to hear what you think of Rayne and Maeve's journey.

Warmest wishes

Fi

PS: I really loved Simon giving Tara, from the previous book, Russian dolls for Christmas!

MIDWIFE'S MISTLETOE BABY

BY
FIONA McARTHUR

First published in Great Britain 2014
by Mills & Boon, an imprint of Harlequin (UK) Limited,
Large Print edition 2015
Eton House, 18-24 Paradise Road,
Richmond, Surrey, TW9 1SR

© 2014 Fiona McArthur

ISBN: 978-0-263-25481-5

Harlequin (UK) Limited's policy is to use papers that are natural, renewable and recyclable products and made from wood grown in sustainable forests. The logging and manufacturing processes conform to the legal environmental regulations of the country of origin.

Printed and bound in Great Britain
by CPI Antony Rowe, Chippenham, Wiltshire

Mother to five sons, **Fiona McArthur** is an Australian midwife who loves to write. Mills & Boon® Medical Romance™ gives Fiona the scope to write about all the wonderful aspects of adventure, romance, medicine and midwifery that she feels so passionate about—as well as an excuse to travel! Now that her boys are older, Fiona and her husband, Ian, are off to meet new people, see new places, and have wonderful adventures. Fiona's website is at www.fionamcarthurauthor.com

Recent titles by Fiona McArthur:

CHRISTMAS WITH HER EX
GOLD COAST ANGELS: TWO TINY HEARTBEATS
THE PRINCE WHO CHARMED HER
A DOCTOR, A FLING & A WEDDING RING
SYDNEY HARBOUR HOSPITAL:
   MARCO'S TEMPTATION
FALLING FOR THE SHEIKH SHE SHOULDN'T
SURVIVAL GUIDE TO DATING YOUR BOSS
HARRY ST CLAIR: ROGUE OR DOCTOR?
MIDWIFE, MOTHER…ITALIAN'S WIFE
MIDWIFE IN THE FAMILY WAY
MIDWIFE IN A MILLION

These books are also available in eBook format from www.millsandboon.co.uk

Dedication

Dedicated to my darling husband, Ian.
Because I love you
xx Fiona

Praise for
Fiona McArthur:

'CHRISTMAS WITH HER EX is everything
a good medical romance should be,
and it tells a story which resonates with
everything Christmas stands for.'
—*HarlequinJunkie*

'McArthur does full justice to an intensely
emotional scene of the delivery of a stillborn
baby—one that marks a turning point in both
the characters' outlooks. The entire story is
liberally spiced with drama, heartfelt emotion
and just a touch of humour.'
—*RT Book Reviews* on
SURVIVAL GUIDE TO DATING YOUR BOSS

'MIDWIFE IN A MILLION
by Fiona McArthur will leave readers
full of exhilaration. Ms McArthur has
created characters that any reader
could fall in love with.'
—*CataRomance*

PROLOGUE

March

RAYNE WALTERS BREATHED a sigh of relief as he passed through immigration and then customs at Sydney airport, deftly texted—I'm through—and walked swiftly towards the exit. Simon would be quick to pick him up. Very efficient was Simon.

He'd had that feeling of disaster closing in since the hiccough at LA when he'd thought he'd left it too late. But the customs officers had just hesitated and then frowned at him and waved him through.

He needed to get to Simon, the one person he wanted to know the truth, before it all exploded in his face. Hopefully not until he made it back to the States. Though they were the same age, and the same height, Simon was like a brother and mentor when he'd needed to make life choices for good rather than fast decisions.

But this choice was already made. He just wanted it not to come as a shock to the one other person whose good opinion mattered. He wasn't looking forward to Simon's reaction, and there would be anger, but the steps were already in motion.

A silver car swung towards him. There he was. He lifted his hand and he could see Simon's smile as he pulled over.

'Good to see you, mate.'

'You too.' They'd never been demonstrative, Rayne had found it too hard——but their friendship in Simon's formative years had been such a light in his grey days, and a few hilarious hell-bent nights, so that just seeing Simon made him feel better.

They pulled out into the traffic and his friend

spoke without looking at him. 'So what's so urgent you need to fly halfway around the world you couldn't tell me on the phone? I can't believe you're going back tomorrow morning.'

Rayne glanced at the heavy traffic and decided this mightn't be a good time to distract Simon with his own impending disaster. Or was that just an excuse to put off the moment? 'Can we wait till we get to your place?'

He watched Simon frown and then nod. 'Sure. Though Maeve's there. She's just had a breakup so I hope a sister in my house won't cramp your style.'

Maeve. Little Maeve, Geez. It was good to think of someone other than himself for a minute. She'd been hot as a teenager and he could imagine she'd be drop-dead gorgeous by now. All of Simon's sisters were but he'd always had a soft spot for Maeve, the youngest. He'd bet, didn't know why, that Maeve had a big front of confidence when, in fact, he'd suspected she was a lot softer than the rest of the strong females in the house.

Though there'd been a few tricky moments when she'd made sure he knew she fancied him—not politic when you were years older than her. He'd got pretty good at not leaving Simon's side while Maeve had been around. 'I haven't seen Maeve for maybe ten years. She was probably about fifteen and a self-assured little miss then.'

'Most of the time she is. Still a marshmallow underneath, though. But she makes me laugh.'

She'd made Rayne laugh too, but he'd never mentioned his avoidance techniques to Simon. He doubted Simon would have laughed at that. Rayne knew Simon thrived on protecting his sisters. It had never been said but the *Keep away from my sisters* sign was clearly planted between them. And Rayne respected that.

'How are your parents?' It was always odd, asking, because he'd only had his mum, and

Simon had two sets of parents. Simon's father, who Rayne had known as a kid, had turned out to be Simon's stepdad and he remembered very well how bitter Simon had been about all the lies. Bitter enough to change his last name.

But Simon's mum had chosen to go with someone she'd thought could give her accidental child the life she wanted him to have, and had been very happy with Simon's wealthy stepdad. Simon's birth father hadn't known of his son's existence until Simon had accidentally found out and gone looking for him.

No such fairy-tale for himself. 'Your father is dead and not worth crying over,' was all his mother had ever said.

'You know Dad and Mum moved to Boston?' Simon's voice broke into his thoughts. 'Dad's bypass went well and Mum's keeping us posted.'

'Good stuff.' Rayne glanced at his friend and enjoyed the smile that lit Simon's face. Funnily, he'd never been jealous of Simon's solid family background. Just glad that he could count this man as his friend and know he wouldn't be judged. Except maybe in the next half-hour when he broke the news.

Simon went on. 'And Angus and the Lyrebird Lake contingent are great. I saw them all at Christmas.' More smiles. He was glad it had all worked out for Simon.

Then the question Rayne didn't want. 'And your mum? She been better since you moved her out to live with you?' Another glance his way and he felt his face freeze as Simon looked at him.

'Fine.' If he started there then the whole thing would come out in the car and he just needed a few more minutes of soaking up the good vibes.

Instead, they talked about work.

About Simon's antenatal breech clinic he was running at Sydney Central. He'd uncovered a passion for helping women avoid unnecessary

Caesareans for breech babies when possible and was becoming one of the leaders in re-establishing the practice of experienced care for normal breech births.

'So how's your job going?' Simon looked across. 'Still the dream job, making fistloads of money doing what you love?'

'Santa Monica's great. The house is finished and looking great.' Funny how unimportant that was in the big picture. 'My boss wants me to think about becoming one of the directors on the board.' That wouldn't happen now. He shook that thought off for later.

'The operating rooms there are state-of-the-art and we're developing a new procedure for cleft pallet repair that's healing twice as fast.'

'You still doing the community work on Friday down at South Central?'

'Yep. The kids are great, and we're slipping in one case a week as a teaching case into the OR in Santa Monica.' He didn't even want to think about letting the kids down there but he did have a very promising registrar he was hoping he could talk to, and who could possibly take over, before it all went down.

They turned off the airport link road and in less than five minutes were driving into Simon's garage. Simon lived across the road from the huge expanse of Botany Bay Rayne had just flown in over. He felt his gut kick with impending doom. Another huge jet flew overhead as the automatic garage door descended and that wasn't all that was about to go down.

He'd be on one of those jets heading back to America tomorrow morning. Nearly thirty hours' flying for one conversation. But, then, he'd have plenty of time to sit around when he got back.

Simon ushered him into the house and through into the den as he called out to his sister. 'We're back.'

Her voice floated down the stairs. 'Getting

dressed.' Traces of the voice he remembered with a definite womanly depth to it and the melody of it made him smile.

'Drink?' Simon pointed to the tray with whisky glass and decanter and Rayne nodded. He'd had two on the plane. Mostly he'd avoided alcohol since med school but he felt the need for a shot to stiffen his spine for the conversation ahead.

'Thanks.' He crossed the room and poured a finger depth. Waved the bottle in Simon's direction. 'You?'

'Nope. I'm not technically on call but my next breech mum is due any day now. I'll have the soda water to keep you company.' Rayne poured him a glass of the sparkling water from the bar fridge.

They sat down. Rayne lifted his glass. 'Good seeing you.' And it was all about to change.

'You too. Now, what's this about?'

Rayne opened his mouth just as Simon's

mobile phone vibrated with an incoming call. Damn. Instead, he took a big swallow of his drink.

Simon frowned at him. Looked at the caller, shrugged his inability to ignore it, and stood up to take the call.

Rayne knew if it hadn't been important he wouldn't have answered. Stared down into the dregs of the amber fluid in his glass. Things happened. Shame it had to happen now. That was his life.

'Sorry, Rayne. I have to go. That's my patient with the breech baby. I said I'd be there. Back as soon as I can.' He glanced at the glass. 'Go easy. I'll still be your mate, no matter what it is.'

Rayne put the glass down. 'Good luck.' With that! He had no doubt about Simon's professional skill. But he doubted he'd be happy with his friend when he knew.

Rayne watched Simon walk from the room

and he was still staring pensively at the door two minutes later when the woman of his dreams sashayed in and the world changed for ever.

One moment. That was all it took. Nothing could have warned him what was about to happen or have prevented him, after one shell-shocked moment, standing up. Not all the disasters in the universe mattered as he walked towards the vision little Maeve had become.

A siren. Calling him without the need for actual words. Her hair loose, thick black waves dancing on her shoulders, and she wore some floating, shimmering, soft shift of apricot that allowed a tantalising glimpse of amazing porcelain cleavage—and no bra, he was pretty sure. A flash of delicious thigh, and then covered again in deceptive modesty. He could feel his heart pound in his throat. Tried to bring it all back to normality but he couldn't. Poleaxed by not-so-little Maeve.

* * *

Maeve paused before entering the room. Drew a breath. She'd spent the day getting ready for this moment. Hair. Nails. Last-minute beauty appointments that had filled the day nicely. When Simon had told her yesterday that Rayne was coming she'd felt her spirits lift miraculously. Gone was the lethargy of self-recriminations from the last month. She really needed to get over that ridiculous inferiority complex she couldn't seem to shake as the youngest of four high achieving girls.

Here was one man who had never disappointed her. Even though she'd been embarrassingly eager to pester him as a gawky teenager, he'd always made her feel like a princess, and she wanted to look her best. Feel good about herself. Get on with her life after the last fiasco and drop all those stupid regrets that were doing her head in.

She hoped he hadn't changed. She'd hero-worshiped the guy since the day he'd picked up the lunch box she'd dropped the first time she'd seen him. Her parents' reservations about Rayne's background and bad-boy status had only made him more irresistible. At fifteen, twenty had been way out of her reach in age.

Well, things should be different this time and she was going to make sure they were at least on an even footing!

Maybe that's where the trill of excitement was coming from and she could feel the smile on her face from anticipation as she stepped into view.

That was the last sane thought. A glance across a room, a searing moment of connection that had her pinned in the doorway so that she stopped and leant against the architrave, suddenly in need of support—a premonition that maybe she'd be biting off more than she could chew even flirting with Rayne. This black-shirted, open-collared hunk was no pretty boy she could order around. And yet it was still Rayne.

He rose and stepped towards her, a head taller than her, shoulders like a front-row forward, and those eyes. Black pools of definite appreciation as he crossed the room in that distinctive prowl of a walk he'd always had until he stood beside her.

A long slow smile. 'Are you here to ruin my life even more?'

God. That voice. Her skin prickled. Could feel her eyebrows lift. Taking in the glory of him. 'Maybe. Maybe I'm the kind of ruin you've been searching for?'

Goodness knew where those words had come from but they slid from her mouth the way her lunch box had dropped from her fingers around ten years ago. The guy was jaw-droppingly gorgeous. And sexy as all get-out!

'My, my. Look at little Maeve.'

And look at big Rayne. Her girl parts quivered.

'Wow!' His voice was low, amused and definitely admiring—and who didn't like someone admiring?—and the pleasure in the word tickled her skin like he'd brushed her all over. Felt impending kismet again. Felt his eyes glide, not missing a thing.

She looked up. Mesmerised. Skidded away from the eyes—too amazing, instead appreciated the black-as-night hair, that strong nose and determined jaw, and those shoulders that blocked her vision of the world. A shiver ran through her. She was like a lamb beckoning to the wolf.

Another long slow smile that could have melted her bra straps if she'd had one on, then he grew sexy-serious. 'Haven't you grown into a beautiful woman? I think we should meet all over again.' A tilt of those sculpted lips and he held out his hand. 'I'm Rayne. And you are?'

Moistened her lips. 'Maeve.' Pretended her throat wasn't as dry as a desert. Held out her own hand and he took her fingers and kissed above her knuckles smoothly so that she sucked her breath in.

Then he allowed her hand to fall. 'Maeve.' The way he said it raised the hair on her arms again. Like ballet dancers *en pointe*. 'Did you know your name means *she who intoxicates*? I read that somewhere, but not until this moment did I believe it.'

She should have laughed and told him he was corny but she was still shaking like a star-struck mute. Finally she retaliated. 'Rain. As in wet?'

He laughed. 'Rayne as in R.A.Y.N.E. My mother hated me.'

'How is your mother?'

His eyes flickered. 'Fine.' Then he seemed to shake off whatever had distracted him and his smile was slow and lethal. 'Would you like to have a drink with me?'

And of course she said, 'Yes!'

She watched him cross the room to Simon's bar and that made her think, only for a milli-second, about her brother. 'Where's Simon?' Thank goodness her brother hadn't seen that explosion of instant lust between them or he'd be playing bomb demolition expert as soon as he cottoned on.

'His breech lady has gone into labour and he's meeting her at the hospital.'

Maeve ticked that obstacle out of the way. A good hour at least but most probably four. She was still languid with residual oxytocin from the Rayne storm as she sank onto the lounge. Then realised she probably should have sat in Simon's favourite chair, opposite, because if Rayne sat next to her here she doubted she'd be able to keep her hands off him.

He sat down next to her and the force field between them glowed like the lights on the run-way across the bay. He handed her a quarter-glass of whisky and toasted her with his own.

Their fingers touched and sizzled and their eyes clashed as they sipped.

'Curiouser and curiouser,' he drawled, and smiled full into her face.

OMG. She licked her lips again and he leaned and took her glass from her hand again and put it down on the coffee table. 'You really shouldn't do that.' Then lifted his finger and gently brushed her bottom lip with aching slowness as he murmured, 'I've been remiss.'

He was coming closer. 'In what way?' *Who owned that breathy whisper?*

'I didn't kiss my old friend hello.' And his face filled her vision and she didn't make any protest before his lips touched, returned and then scorched hers.

In those first few seconds of connection she could feel a leashed desperation about him that she didn't understand, because they had plenty of time, an hour at least, but then all thoughts fled as sensation swamped her.

Rayne's mouth was like no other mouth she'd ever known. Hadn't even dreamt about. Like velvet steel, smoothly tempered with a suede finish, and the crescendo was deceptively gradual as it steered them both in a sensual duel of lips and tongue and inhalation of whisky breath into a world that beckoned like a light at the end of the tunnel. She hadn't even known there was a tunnel!

Everything she'd imagined could be out there beckoned and promised so much more. She wanted more, desperately needed more, and lifted her hands to clasp the back of his head, revel in his thick wavy hair sliding through her fingers as she pulled him even closer.

His hands slid down her ribs, across her belly and up under and then circling her breasts through the thin fabric of her silk overshirt. His fingers tightened in deliciously powerful appreciation then he pulled away reluctantly.

'Silk? I'd hate to spoil this so I'd better stop.'

'I'll buy another one,' she murmured against his lips.

Rayne forced his hands to draw back. It was supposed to be a hello kiss. Holy hell, what was he doing? He'd barely spoken to the woman in ten years and his next stop was definitely lower down. They'd be naked on the floor before he realised it if he didn't watch out. 'Maybe we should draw a breath?'

She sat back with a little moue of disappointment, followed by one of those delicious tip-of-the-tongue lip-checks that drove him wild. He was very tempted to throw caution to the winds, and her to the floor, and have his wicked way with the siren. Then he saw Simon's glass of sparkling water sitting forlornly on the table and remembered his unspoken promise. Forced himself to sit back. He'd be better having a cold glass of water himself.

'I'm starving!' He wasn't, but appealing to a woman's need to feed a man was always a good ploy to slow the world down.

She shrugged and he wanted to laugh out loud. Still a princess. Gloriously a princess. 'Kitchen's through there.' A languid hand in vague direction. 'I'm not much of a cook but you could make yourself something.'

Observed her eyes skid away from his. Decided she was lying. 'Don't you know the way to a man's heart is through his stomach?'

'And the way to a woman's heart is more of that hello kissing.' She sighed and stood up. 'But come on, I'll feed you. And then I'm going to kiss you again before my brother comes home. You'll owe me.'

He did laugh at that. 'I'll pay what I have to pay.' And he thought, I am not sleeping with this woman but thank God I brought condoms.

Maeve had lied about not being able to cook. She'd done French, Italian and Spanish culinary courses, could make anything out of nothing, and Simon's fridge was definitely not made up of nothing. 'Spanish omelette, French salad and garlic pizza bread?'

'Hold the garlic pizza bread.'

She grinned at him, starting to come down from the deluge of sensations that had saturated her brain. She'd planned on being admired, building her self-esteem with a safe yet sexy target, not ending up in bed with the guy. 'Good choice.' Heard the words and decided they applied to herself as well. It would be a good choice not to end up in bed either.

Then set about achieving a beautifully presented light meal perfect for a world traveller just off a plane.

'Oh, my.' He glanced down at his plate in awe. 'She cooks well.'

'Only when I feel like it.' And spun away, but he caught her wrist. Lifted it to his mouth and kissed the delicate inside skin once, twice, three times, and Maeve thought she was going to swoon. She tugged her hand free because she needed to think and she hadn't stopped *feeling* since she'd seen this man. She mimicked him. 'He kisses well.'

He winked at her. 'Only when he feels like it.'

She leaned into him. 'We'll work on that. Eat your dinner like a good boy.' *While I get some distance, fan my face and figure out why I'm acting like he's my chance at salvation. Or is that damnation?*

Five minutes later Rayne sat back from his empty plate. He had been hungry. Or the food was too good to possibly leave. 'Thank you.'

He needed a strategy of space between him and this woman. What the heck was going on to cause this onslaught of attraction between them? His own dire circumstances? The thought that she might be the last beautiful thing he would see or touch for a long time?

And her? Well, she was vulnerable. Simon had suggested that. But vulnerable wasn't the word he would have used. Stunning, intoxicating, black-widow dangerous?

He stood up and put his plate in the sink. Rinsed it, like he always did because he'd been responsible for any cleaning he'd wanted done for a long time, and internally he smiled because she didn't say, *Leave that, I'll do it*, like most women would have. She leant on the doorframe and watched him do it.

'Simon said you've just finished a relationship?' Seemed like his subconscious wanted to get to the bottom of it because his conscious mind hadn't been going to ask that question.

'Hmm. It didn't end well, and I've been a dishrag poor Simon had to put up with for the last month. You've no idea the lift I got when Simon said you were coming.'

No subterfuge there. He had the feeling she didn't know the meaning of the word. 'Thank you. But you know I'm here only for one night. I fly back tomorrow.'

She turned her head to look at him. 'Do you have to?'

That was ironic. 'No choice.' Literally. 'And I won't be back for a long time.' A very long time maybe.

She nodded. 'Then we'd best make the most of tonight.'

He choked back a laugh. 'What on earth can you mean?'

'Catch up on what we've both been doing, of course. Before Simon monopolises you.' She was saying one thing but her body was saying something else as she sashayed into the lounge again, and he may as well have had a leash around his neck because he followed her with indecent haste and growing fatalism.

'Simon will be back soon.' A brief attempt to return to reality but she was standing in the centre of the room looking suddenly unsure, and that brief fragility pierced him like no other re-action could have. Before he knew it he had his arms around her, cradling her against his chest, soothing the black hair away from her face. Silk skin, glorious cheekbones, a determined little chin. And she felt so damn perfect in his arms as she snuggled into him.

'Take me to bed, Rayne. Make me feel like a woman again.'

'That would be too easy.' He kissed her fore-head. 'I don't think that's a good idea, sweet-heart.'

'I'm a big girl, Rayne. Covered for contra-ception. Unattached and in sound mind. Do I have to beg?'

He looked at her, squeezed her to him. Thought about the near future and how he would never get this chance again because things would never be the same. He would never be the same. Searched her face for any change of mind. No. Bloody hell. She didn't have to beg.

So he picked her up in his arms, and she lifted her hands to clasp him around his neck, and he kissed her gorgeous mouth and they lost a few more minutes in a hazy dream of connection. Finally he got the words out. 'So which bedroom is yours?'

She laughed. 'Up two flights of stairs. Want me to walk?'

'Much as I have enjoyed watching you walk, I'd prefer to carry you.'

And with impressive ease he did. Maeve rested her head back on that solid shoulder and gazed up at the chiselled features and strong nose. And those sinful lips. OMG, did she know what she was doing? Well, there was no way she wanted this to stop. This chemistry had been building since that first searing glance that had jerked and stunned them both like two people on the same elastic. She tightened her hands around his neck.

He felt so powerful—not pretty and perfect like Sean had been—but she didn't want to think about Sean. About the pale comparison of a man she'd wasted her heart on when she should have always known Rayne would stand head and shoulders above any other man.

Speaking of shoulders, he used one to push open the door she indicated, knocked it shut with his foot, and strode across the room to the big double bed she thought he would toss her onto, but he smiled, glanced around the room and lowered her gently until her feet were on the floor.

His breathing hadn't changed and he looked as if he could have done it all again without working a sweat.

Ooh la la. 'I'm impressed.'

He raised his brows quizzically and freed the French drapes until they floated down to cover the double window in a flounced bat of their lacy eyelids and the room dimmed to a rosy glow from the streetlights outside. Slid his wallet out of his pocket and put it on the windowsill after retrieving a small foil packet.

Then he pulled her towards him and spun her until her spine was against the wall and her breasts were pressed into his hardness. Shook his head and smiled full into her eyes. Felt her knees knock as he said, 'You are the sexiest woman I have ever seen.'

She thought, *And you are the sexiest man*, as she lifted her lips to his, and thank goodness he didn't wait to be asked twice. Like falling into a swirling maelstrom of luscious sensation, Maeve felt reality disappear like a leaf sucked into a drainpipe then she heard him say something. Realised he'd created physical distance between them. Her mind struggled to process sound to speech.

'Miss Maeve, are you sure you want to proceed?'

It was a jolting and slightly disappointing

thing to say in the bubble of sensuality he'd created and she looked up at him. Surprised a look of anguish she hadn't expected. 'Are you trying to spoil this for a particular reason?'

A distance she didn't like flashed in his eyes. 'Maybe.'

She pulled his head forward with her hands in his hair. 'Well, don't!'

Rayne shrugged, smiled that lethal smile of his, and instead he lifted her silk shift over her head in a slow sexy exposure, leaving the covering camisole and the dark shadow of her breasts plainly visible through it.

He trailed the backs of his fingers up the sides of her chest and she shivered, wanted him to rip it off so she could feel his hands on her skin. And he knew it.

This time the backs of his fingers trailed down and caught the hem of the camisole, catching the final layer, leaving her top half naked to the air on her sensitised skin.

She heard him suck in his breath, heard it catch in his throat as he glimpsed her body for the first time—and the tiny peach G-string that was all that was left.

Her turn. He had way too many clothes on and she needed to look and feel his skin with a sudden hunger she had no control over.

She reached up and danced her fingers swiftly down the fastening of his black shirt, as if un-buttoning for the Olympics way ahead of any other competitor, because she'd never felt such urgency to slip her hands inside a man's shirt. Never wanted to connect as badly as now with the taut skin-covered muscle and bone of a man. The man.

This was Rayne. The Rayne. And he felt as fabulous as she'd known he would and the faster she did this the faster he would kiss her again. Her fingers seemed to glow wherever she touched and she loved the heat between them like a shivering woman loved a fire.

While her fingers were gliding with relish he'd unzipped and was kicking away his trousers. They stood there, glued together, two layers of mist-like fabric between their groins, two flimsy, ineffectual barriers that only inflamed them more, and his mouth recommenced its onslaught and she was lost.

Until he shifted. Moved that wicked mouth and tongue lower, a salutation of her chin, her neck, her collarbone, a slow, languorous, teasing circle around her breast and exquisite tantalising pleasure she'd never imagined engulfed her as he took the rosy peak and flicked it with delicate precision.

She gasped.

His hands encircled her ribs, the strong thumbs pushing her breasts into perky attention for his favours. Peaks of sensitive supplication and he took advantage until she was writhing, aching for him, helpless against the wall at her back, unable to be silent.

She. Could. Not. Get. Enough.

Rayne lifted his head, heard the moan of a woman enthralled, saw the wildness in her eyes, felt his own need soar to meet hers, dropped his hands to the lace around her hips and slid those wicked panties slowly down her legs, savoured the silk of her skin, the tautness of her thighs under his fingers, and then the scrap of material fell in a ridiculously tiny heap at her feet. There was something so incredibly sinful about that fluttering puddle of fabric, and he'd bet he'd think about it later, many times, as he reached for the condom and dropped his own briefs swiftly.

Then his hands slid back to her buttocks. Those round globes of perfection that fitted his hands perfectly. Felt the weight of her, lifted, supported her body in his hands, and the power of that feeling expanded with the strain in his arms and exultantly, slowly, her back slid up the wall and she rose to meet him.

Rayne slowly and relentlessly pinned her with his body and she wrapped her legs around him the way he had known, instinctively, she would, and it felt as incredible as he'd also known it could be, except it was more. So much more. And they began to dance the ancient dance of well-matched mates.

The rising sun striped the curtains with a golden beam of new light and Maeve awoke in love. Some time in the night it had come to her and it was as indestructible as a glittering diamond in her chest. How had that happened?

Obviously she'd always loved him.

And it was nothing like the feelings she'd had for other men. This was one hundred per cent 'you light my fire, I know you would cherish me if you loved me back, I want to have babies with you' love. So it looked like she'd have to pack her bags and follow the man to the States.

At least her mother lived there.

But Rayne was gone from their tumbled bed and someone was talking loudly downstairs.

Maeve sat up amidst the pillows he'd packed around her, realised she was naked and slightly stiff, began to smile and then realised the loud voice downstairs was Simon's.

A minute later she'd thrown a robe over her nakedness and hurried into Simon's study, where two burly federal policemen had Rayne in…handcuffs?

The breath jammed in her throat and she leant against the doorframe that had supported her last night. Needed it even more now.

Simon was saying, 'What the hell? Rayne? This has to be a mistake.'

'No mistake. Just didn't get time to explain.' Rayne glanced across as Maeve entered and shut his eyes for a moment as if seeing her just made everything worse. Not how she wanted to be remembered by him.

Then his thick lashes lifted as he stared. 'Bye, Maeve,' looked right through her and then away.

Simon glanced between the two, dawning suspicion followed swiftly by disbelief and then anger. 'So you knew they'd come and you...' He couldn't finish the sentence. Sent Maeve an, 'I'll talk to you later' look, but the federal policemen were already nudging Rayne towards the door.

Simon was still in the clothes he'd left in last night so he hadn't been home long. Rayne was fully dressed, again in sexy black, and shaved, had his small cabin bag, so it looked like he'd been downstairs, waiting. She would never know if it was for Simon or the police.

She wondered whether the police hadn't come he would have woken her to say goodbye. The obvious negative left her feeling incredibly cold in the belly after the conflagration they'd shared last night and her epiphany this morning.

He'd said he was going and wouldn't be back for a while but she'd never imagined this scenario.

Then he really was gone and Simon was shaking his head.

CHAPTER ONE

Nine months later.
Looking for Maeve.

RAYNE'S MOTHER DIED of a heroin overdose on the fifteenth of December. He was released from prison the day after, when the posted envelope of papers arrived at the Santa Monica police station, and he put his head in his hands at his inability to save her. The authorities hadn't been apologetic—he should have proclaimed his innocence, but he'd just refused to speak.

Her last written words to him…

My Rayne
I love you. You are my shining star. I would never have survived in prison but it

seems I can't survive on the outside either with you in there. I'm so sorry it took me so long to fix it.

With the other letter and proof of her guilt she'd kept, the charges on Rayne were dropped and he buried her a week later in Santa Monica. It had been the only place she'd known some happiness, and it was fine to leave her there in peace.

He had detoured to see his old boss, who had been devastated by the charges against him, explained briefly that he'd known she wouldn't survive in jail, and the man promised to start proceedings for the restoration of his licence to practise. Undo what damage he could, and as he'd been able to keep most of the sensation out of the papers, that was no mean offer.

Then Rayne gave all his mother's clothes and belongings to the Goodwill Society and ordered her the biggest monumental angel he could for the top of her grave. It would have made her smile.

Then he put the house up for sale and bought a ticket for Australia and Maeve. The woman he couldn't forget after just one night. Not because he was looking for happily ever after but because he owed it to her and Simon to explain. And if he was going to start a new life he had to know what was left of his old one. If anything.

All he knew was the man he was now was no fit partner for Maeve and he had no doubt Simon would say the same.

On arrival it had taken him two days of dogged investigation before he'd traced Maeve to Lyrebird Lake and he would have thought of it earlier if he'd allowed himself to think of Simon first.

Simon's birth father lived there and Simon often spent Christmas with them—he should have remembered that. With Maeve's mother in the US it made sense she was with her brother.

Who knew if she'd say yes to seeing him after the way he'd left, if either of them would? He guessed he couldn't blame them when they didn't know the facts, but he had to know they were both all right. Maybe he should have opened the letters Maeve had sent and not refused the phone calls Simon had tried, but staying isolated from others and keeping the outside world out of his head had been the only way he'd got through it.

Looked down at the wad of letters in his hand and decided against opening the letters now in case she refused to see him in writing.

Two hundred miles away from Lyrebird Lake, and driving just over the legal speed limit, Rayne pressed a little harder on the accelerator pedal. The black Chev, a souped-up version of his first car from years ago, throttled back with a throaty grumble.

He didn't even know if Maeve had a partner, had maybe even married, but he had to find out. She would refuse to see him. It was ridiculous to be propelled on with great urgency when it had been so long, but he was. He should wait until after the holiday season but he couldn't.

The picture in his head of her leaning against the doorframe as he'd been led away had tortured him since that night. The fact that he'd finally discovered the woman he needed to make him whole had been there all the time in his past, and he'd let her down in the most cowardly way by not telling her what would happen.

He couldn't forgive himself so how did he think that Maeve and her brother would forgive him? All he just knew was he had to find her and explain. Try to explain.

So clearly he remembered her vulnerability before he'd carried her up those stairs. Blindingly he saw her need to see herself the way he saw her. Perhaps it was too late.

If she had moved on, then he would have to go, but he needed her to know the fault was all his before they said a final goodbye. It wasn't too late to at least tell her she couldn't have been more perfect on that night all those months ago.

A police highway patrol car passed in the opposite direction. The officer glanced across at him and Rayne slowed. Stupid. To arrive minutes later after nine months wouldn't make the difference but if he was pulled over for speeding then the whole catastrophe could start again. International drivers licence. Passports. He didn't want the hassle.

It was lucky the salesman had filled the fuel tank last night because he'd only just realised it was early Christmas morning. Every fuel stop was shut. He had no food or drinks except the water he'd brought with him. Big deal except he was gatecrashing Simon's family at a time visitors didn't usually drop in. Hopefully the rest of the family weren't assembled when he arrived.

It wasn't the first time he'd done this. He remembered Simon taking him home to his other parents' one year while they'd been in high school. Rayne's mother had ended up in rehab over the holiday break, it had always been the hardest time of the year for her to stay straight, and his friend, Simon, had come to check on him.

He'd been sixteen and sitting quietly watching television when Simon had knocked at the door, scolded him for not letting him know, and dragged him reluctantly back to his house for the best Christmas he'd ever had.

Simon's parents had ensured he'd had a small Christmas sack at the end of his bed on Christmas morning and Maeve had made him a card and given him a Cellophane bag of coconut ice she'd made for everyone that year. He'd loved the confectionary ever since.

Well, here he was again, gatecrashing. Unwanted.

It was anything but funny. The truly ridiculous part was that in his head he'd had an unwilling relationship with Maeve for the last nine months. She'd made an irreversible imprint on him in those hours he'd held her in his arms. Blown him away, and he was still in pieces from it. He'd kept telling himself they'd only connected in his last desperate attempt to hold onto someone good before the bad came but he had no doubt she would always hold a sacred piece of his heart.

In prison he'd separated his old life out of his head. Had kept it from being contaminated by his present. Refused any visitors and stored the mail. But when his defences had been down, when he'd drifted off to sleep, Maeve had slid in beside him, been with him in the morning when he'd woken up, and at night when he'd dreamt. He'd had no control over that.

But he'd changed. Hardened. Couldn't help being affected by the experience, and she didn't need a man like he'd become—so he doubted he'd stay. Just explain and then head back to Sydney to sort out his life. Start fresh when he could find some momentum for beginning. Wasn't even sure he would return to paediatrics. Felt the need for something physical. Something to use up the coil of explosive energy he'd been accumulating over the last nine months.

So maybe he'd go somewhere in between for a while where he could just soak up nature and the great outdoors now that he had the freedom to enjoy it.

Funny how things were never as important until you couldn't have them. He'd lusted after a timeless rainforest, or a deserted mountain stream, or a lighthouse with endless ocean to soothe his soul.

Or Maeve, a voice whispered. No.

CHAPTER TWO

Maeve

MAEVE PATTED HER round and rolling belly to soothe the child within. Christmas in Lyrebird Lake. She should have been ecstatic and excited about the imminent birth of her baby.

Ecstatic about the fact that only yesterday Simon had declared his love to Tara and was engaged to a woman she couldn't wait to call her sister. She put her fingers over the small muscle at the corner of her eye, which was twitching. But instead she was a mess.

Her only brother, or half-brother, she supposed she should acknowledge that, seeing she was living in Lyrebird Lake where his birth father lived, was engaged to be married. That was very exciting news.

And it wasn't like Simon's family hadn't made her welcome. But it wasn't normal to land on people who didn't know you for one of the biggest moments of your life even if Simon had always raved about Lyrebird Lake.

The place was worth raving about. She'd never been so instantly received for who she was, even in her own family, she thought with a tinge of uneasy disloyalty, but that explained why Simon had always been the least judgemental of all her siblings.

Until she'd slept with Rayne, that was.

Simon's other family didn't know the meaning of the word judgmental. Certainly less than her mother, but that was the way mum was, and she accepted that.

And she and Simon had re-established some of their previous closeness, mostly thanks to Tara.

The fabulous Tara. Her new friend and personal midwife was a doll and she couldn't imagine anyone she would rather have in the family.

She, Maeve, was an absolute bitch to be depressed by the news but it was so hard to see them so happy when she was so miserable.

She gave herself a little mental shake. Stop it.

Glanced out the window to the manger on the lawn. It was Christmas morning, and after nearly four weeks of settling in there was no place more welcoming or peaceful to have her baby.

So what was wrong with her?

It was all very well being a midwife, knowing what was coming, but she had this mental vision of her hand being held and it wasn't going to be Simon's. Have her brother, in the room while she laboured? Not happening, even if he was an obstetrician.

No. It would be Tara's hand that steadied her,

which was good but not what she'd secretly and hopelessly dreamt of.

That scene she'd replayed over in her head a thousand times, him crossing the floor to her after that first glance, and later the feel of his arms around her as he'd carried her so easily up the stairs, the absolutely incredible dominance yet tenderness of his lovemaking. Gooseflesh shimmered on her arms.

She shook her head. The birth would be fine. It was okay.

She tried to shake the thought of needing Rayne to get through labour from her mind but it clung like a burr and refused to budge as if caught in the whorls of her cerebral convolutions.

Which was ridiculous because the fact was Rayne didn't want her.

He'd refused to answer her letters or take the call the one time she'd tried to call the prison, had had to go through the horror of finding out his prison number, been transferred to another section, the interminable wait and then the coldness of his refusal to speak to her.

Obviously he didn't want her!

Simon had told her he'd found out he would be in prison for at least two years, maybe even five, and that the charges had been drug related. She, for one, still didn't believe it.

But she hated the fact Rayne didn't want to see her.

Her belly tightened mildly in sympathy, like it had been tightening for the last couple of weeks every now and then, and she patted the taut, round bulge. *It's okay, baby. Mummy will be sensible. She'll get over your father one day.* But that wasn't going to happen if she stayed here mooning.

Maeve sat up and eased her legs out of the bed until her feet were on the floor. Grunted quietly with the effort and then smiled ruefully at herself for the noisy exertion of late pregnancy.

She needed to go for a walk. Free her mind outside the room. Stay fit for the most strenuous exertion of her life.

It was time to greet Christmas morning with a smile and a gentle, ambling welcome in the morning air before the Queensland heat glued her to the cool chair under the tree in the back yard. The tables were ready to be set for breakfast and later lunch with Simon's family and she would put on a smiling face.

She wondered if Tara was up yet. Her friend had come in late last night with Simon, she'd heard them laughing quietly and the thought made her smile. Two gorgeous people in love. The smile slipped from her face and she dressed as fast as she could in her unbalanced awkwardness and for once didn't worry about make-up.

Self-pity was weak and she needed to get over herself. She was the lucky one, having a baby when lots of women ached for the chance, and she couldn't wait.

It wasn't as if she didn't have a family who loved her, even if her mum was in the States.

But she had dear Louisa, Simon's tiny but sprightly grandmother, spoiling them all with her old-fashioned country hospitality and simple joy in kinfolk. She, Maeve, was twenty-five and needed to grow up and enjoy simple pleasures like Louisa did.

Once outside, she set off towards the town and the air was still refreshingly cool. Normally she would have walked around the lake but it was Sunday, and Simon liked the Sunday papers. Did they print newspapers on Christmas Day? Would the shop even be open? She hadn't thought of that before she'd left but if it didn't then that was okay.

It was easier not to think in the fresh air and distractions of walking with a watermelon-sized belly out front cleared the self-absorbtion.

Maeve saw the black, low-to-the-ground, old-fashioned utility as it turned into the main street and smiled. A hot rod like you saw at car shows with wide silver wheels and those long red bench seats in the front designed for drive-in movies. It growled down the road like something out of *Happy Days*, she thought to herself. The square lines and rumbling motor made it stand out from the more family-orientated vehicles she usually saw. Something about it piqued her curiosity.

She stared at the profile of the man driving and then her whole world tilted. Shock had her clutching her throat with her fingers and then their eyes met. Her heart suddenly thumped like the engine of the black beast and the utility swerved to the edge of the road and pulled up. The engine stopped and so did her breath—then her chest bumped and she swayed with the shock.

It was Maeve! The connection was instantaneous. Like the first time. But she was different. He blinked. Pregnant! Very pregnant!

Rayne was out of the car and beside her in seconds, saw the colour drain from her face, saw her eyes roll back. He reached her just as she began to crumple. Thank God. She slumped into his arms and he caught her urgently and lifted her back against his chest, felt and smelt the pure sweetness of her hair against his face as he turned, noticed the extra weight of her belly with a grimace as he struggled with the door catch without dropping her. Finally he eased her backwards onto the passenger seat and laid her head gently back along the seat.

He stared at the porcelain beauty of the woman he'd dreamed about throughout that long horrible time of incarceration.

Maeve.

Pregnant by someone else. The hollow bitterness of envy. The swell of fierce emotion and the wish it had been him. He patted her hands, patted her cheek, and slowly she stirred.

Unable to help the impossible dream, he began

to count dates in his head. He frowned. Pushed away a sudden, piercing joy, worked out the dates again. But they'd both used contraception. It couldn't be…

She groaned. Stirred more vigorously. Her glorious long eyelashes fluttered and she opened her eyes. They widened with recognition.

Then she gagged and he reached in and lifted her shoulders so she was sitting on the seat and could gag out the door. She didn't look at him again. Just sat with her shoulders bowed and her head in her hands.

He reached past her to the glove box and removed a small packet of tissues. Nudged her fingers and put them into her hand. She took them, but even after she'd finished wiping her mouth she still didn't look at him and he glanced around the street to see if anyone had noticed. Thank God for quiet Sunday mornings. Quiet Christmas morning, actually.

Well, that was unexpected. Something going right!

Seeing Maeve outside and alone. So unplanned. Looking down at her, he couldn't believe she was here in front of him. His eyes were drawn to the fragile V of the nape of her neck, the black hair falling forward away from the smoothness of her ivory skin, and he realised his heart was thumping like a piston in his chest. Like he'd run a marathon. Like he'd seen a vision of the future that was so bright he was blinded. Fool.

It felt like a dream. A stupid, infantile, Christmas fantasy… In reality, though, the woman of his dreams had, in fact, fainted and then thrown up at the very sight of him! He needed to get a grip.

CHAPTER THREE

After faint...

'WHERE DID YOU come from?' Maeve opened
her eyes. Barely raised her voice because her
throat was closed with sudden tears. She kept
her head down. Couldn't believe she'd fainted
and thrown up as a first impression. Well, he
shouldn't have appeared out of nowhere.

'America. Earlier this week. You're pregnant!'
Der. 'Does Simon know?'

'That you're pregnant?'

She sighed. Her head felt it was going to explode. Not so much with the headache that shimmered behind her eyes but with the thoughts
that were ricocheting around like marbles in

her head. Just what she needed. A smart-alec answer when she had a million questions.

Awkwardly she sat straighter and shifted her bottom on the seat in an attempt to stand. Frustratingly she couldn't get enough purchase until he put his hand down and took hers.

She looked at his brown, manly fingers so much larger than the thin white ones they enclosed. Rayne was here. She could feel the warmth from his skin on hers. Really here.

He squeezed her fingers and then pulled steadily so she floated from the car like a feather from a bottle. She'd forgotten how strong he was. How easily he could move her body around. 'I assume you caught me when everything went black?'

'Thank goodness.' She looked up at the shudder in his voice. 'Imagine if I hadn't.'

She instantly dropped her other hand to her stomach and the baby moved as if to reassure her. Her shoulders drooped again with relief.

'You're pregnant,' he said again.

Now she looked at him. Saw the rampant confusion in a face she'd never seen confusion in before. 'I told you that. In the letters.'

His face shuttered. A long pause. 'I didn't open your letters.'

Maeve was dumbstruck, temporarily unable to speak. He hadn't opened her letters? The hours she'd spent composing and crunching and rewriting and weeping over them before she'd posted them. Wow!

That explained the lack of reply, she thought with a spurt of temper, but it also created huge questions as to just how important she'd been to him. Obviously not very. Not even being locked away in prison had been enough to tempt him to open her letters. She felt the nausea rise again.

He'd refused to talk to Simon too and she knew her brother had been hurt about that. He had hoped for some reassurance from Rayne that somewhere there was an explanation.

The guy was lower than she thought. She needed to protect Simon from being upset a day after his happiest day. That was a real worry. Or a diversion for her mind.

She tried to compose herself, get her thoughts together...

'I don't think you should see Simon until I can warn him you're back.'

Rayne straightened. Lifted his chin. 'I'm not going to hide.'

'It's not about you.' She could feel the unfairness expand in her. This was not how she dreamed their first meeting would be. Why couldn't he have warned her he was coming? Given her a chance to have her defences sorted? Dressed nicely? Put her make-up on, for goodness' sake? She'd just walked out of the house in her expander jeans and a swing top. And trainers. She groaned.

'Are you okay?'

She looked up. Saw the broad shoulders, bulging muscles in his arms, that chest she'd dreamt of for three quarters of a year. He was here and she wanted to be scooped up and cradled against that chest but he wasn't saying the right things. 'You can't see Simon yet. He's just got engaged. He's happy. I won't let you do that. You've upset him enough.'

He'd upset her too, though upset was an understatement. Hurt badly. Devastated. But then you reappeared at the right moment, a tiny voice whispered. The exact right moment. Just in time.

She saw a flicker of pain cross his face and she closed her eyes. What was she doing? Why was she being like this? Was she trying to drive him away?

She needed to think. It overwhelmed her that Rayne was here. As if she'd conjured up him by her need this morning and now she didn't know what she should think. And he hadn't known she was pregnant!

* * *

Rayne was having all sorts of problems keeping his thoughts straight. He could see she was at a loss too. 'Maeve!'

'What?'

He needed to know. Couldn't believe it but didn't want to believe it was someone else. 'Are you pregnant with my baby?'

She hunched her shoulders as if to keep him out. 'It's my baby. You didn't want to know about it.'

He pulled her in close to him and put both arms around her. Lifted her chin to look at him. 'For God's sake, woman.' Resisted the urge to shake her. 'Are you pregnant with my baby?'

'Yes. Now let go of me, Rayne.' His loosened his fingers. Felt her pull away coolly. Create distance between them like a crack from a beautiful glacier breaking away from its mountain, and his heart, a heart that had been a solid rock inside him, cracked too.

Maeve turned her back on him and climbed awkwardly into his car. The realisation that she couldn't protect Simon from this shock forever hit her.

'Come on. Let's get it over with. You need to see Simon and then we need to talk.'

Simon came out of the house when the car pulled up and a petite blonde woman followed him. Rayne remembered now that Maeve had said Simon was engaged. This would be some first introduction.

Rayne climbed out and walked around to open the passenger door; he glanced at his old friend, who looked less than pleased, and then back at the woman's hand he wanted to hold more than anything else in the world.

For an icy moment there he thought she wasn't going to allow him that privilege—right when he needed her most—but then she uncurled her closed fist and allowed her fingers to slide in beside his. By the time Simon had arrived she was standing beside him. Solidarity he hadn't expected.

'They let you out?' There was no Christmas spirit in that statement, Rayne thought sardonically to himself, though couldn't say he could blame him, considering Maeve's condition.

He stared into Simon's face. Felt the coolness between them like an open wound. 'I wanted to explain.' He shrugged. 'It just didn't happen.'

'Instead, you slept with my sister.'

'There's that.' To hell with this.

He just wanted it over. Tell Simon the truth. Let Maeve know at least the father of her baby wasn't a criminal. At the very least. Then get the hell away from here because these people didn't deserve him to infect their live with the disaster that seemed to follow him around.

'When my mother died there wasn't a reason for me to be in there any more. She told them the truth before she overdosed and they dropped the charges.'

Maeve's breath drew in beside him. 'Your mother died?' Felt her hand, a precious hand he'd forgotten he still held, tighten in his. She squeezed his fingers and he looked down at her. Saw the genuine sympathy and felt more upset than he had for the last horrific year. How could she be so quick to feel sorry for him when he'd ruined her life with his own selfishness? That thought hurt even more.

'You took the rap for your mother!' Simon's curt statement wasn't a question. 'Of course you did.' He slapped himself on the forehead. Repeated, 'Of course you did.'

He didn't want to talk about his mother. Didn't want sympathy. He spoke to Simon. 'I understand you not wanting me here.'

He forced himself to let go of Maeve's hand. 'Take Maeve inside. She fainted earlier, though she didn't fall.' He heard Simon's swift intake of breath and saw the blonde woman, from hanging back, shift into gear to swift concern.

He felt Maeve's glance. Her hand brushed the woman's gesture away. 'No. We need to talk.'

'I'll come back later when you've had a chance to rest. I'll find somewhere to stay for tonight.'

And give myself a chance to think, at least, he thought. He reached into his wallet and pulled out a piece of paper on which he'd written his number. 'This is my mobile number. Phone me when you've rested.' And then he spun on his heel and walked away from the lot of them, wishing he had warned them he was coming, though he wasn't sure it would have gone over any better if he had.

Well, they knew the truth now. He'd done what he'd come to do. Learnt something he'd never envisaged and was still grappling with that momentous news. He allowed himself one long sweeping glance over the woman he had dreamed about every night, soaking in the splendour that was Maeve. Her breasts full and ripe for his child, her belly swollen and taut, and her face pale with the distress he'd caused her.

Maeve allowed Tara to steer her back inside, up the hallway to her bedroom, because suddenly she felt as weak as a kitten. Simon was still standing on the street, watching the black utility disappear down the road with a frown on his face, but she'd worry about Simon later.

An almost silent whistle from Tara beside her drew her attention as she sat down on her bed. 'So that's Rayne. Not quite what I imagined. A tad larger than life.' Tara squeezed her arm in sympathy. 'You look pale from shock.'

Maeve grimaced in agreement. Glanced at Tara, calm and methodical as usual as she helped her take off her shoes. 'It was a shock. And highly embarrassing. Not only did I faint but then proceeded to throw up in front of him.'

She felt the assessing glance Tara cast over her. 'For a very pregnant lady you've had a busy morning and it hasn't really started yet.'

It was barely seven o'clock. 'Lucky I got up early. It was supposed to be a gentle Christmas morning walk for Simon's newspaper.'

'The shop won't be open. But your Rayne is a Christmas present with a difference.' Tara laughed. 'What was it you said when you described him to me? A head taller and shoulders like a front-row forward and those dark eyes. No wonder you fell for him, boots and all.'

A fallen woman. And still in love with him, boots and all. 'Is it mad that even after ten minutes with him after all this time, I wanted to go with him? That I feel like we've been together for so much more than one night? That I can even feel that when he's just been away? When even I know that's too simplistic and white-washed.'

She saw Tara look towards the bedside table,

cross to her glass of water and bring it back for her. 'Even from where I was standing, I could feel the energy between you two. I wouldn't be surprised if Simon felt it too.'

'Thanks for that, at least.' She took a sip of water and it did make her feel a little clearer. 'Problem is, I was okay to sleep with but not okay to tell that he was going to prison.'

'Well.' Tara looked thoughtful. 'It seems he has got an explanation if he took the blame for his mother. And things are different now. He can't just walk away and think you'll be better off without him without even discussing it.'

She touched Maeve's shoulder in sympathy. 'And you have been carrying his child. So I guess at least a part of him has been with you since then.' Tara gave her a quick hug. 'He looks tough and self-sufficient but doesn't look a bad man.'

She knew he wasn't. From the bottom of her heart. 'He's not. I believe he's a good man.' She stroked her belly gently. 'I have to believe that if he's going to be part of our lives. And until this…' she patted her belly again '…Simon wouldn't hear a wrong word said about him.' She glanced at Tara and smiled to lighten the dramatic morning. 'And we both know Simon has good taste.'

Tara blushed but brushed that aside. 'Did he say he wants to be a part of your lives?'

In what brief window of opportunity? 'We didn't get that far. What with me fainting like a goose at the sight of him.' Maeve shook her head. Thought about it. 'He said he hadn't opened my mail. That he didn't know I was pregnant.' She thought some more. 'But he didn't look horrified when I told him.'

'Helpful. Though why he wouldn't open your mail has me puzzled.'

Me, too. 'I'll be asking that when he comes back. And it's Christmas morning.' She suddenly thought of the impact of her commotion on everyone else's day. That's what Lyrebird Lake did to you. Made you begin to think more of other people. 'I hope it doesn't spoil your first Christmas with Simon. I feel like I'm gate-crashing your engagement celebrations with my dramas.'

'Nothing can spoil that.' A lovely smile from Tara. 'I'm just glad we're here for you. No better time for family. And Simon will be fine.'

Tara had said family. The idea shone like a star in a dark night sky. It was a good time for family. Tara had probably meant Simon's family but Maeve was thinking of her own. Rayne and her and their baby as a family.

To Maeve it had felt like she'd been marking time for Rayne to arrive and now he was here he was her family. As long as he could handle that idea. Well, he'd just have to get used to it.

She heard Simon's footsteps approaching and as he paused at her bedroom door Maeve felt his assessing glance.

She looked at him. 'Rayne went to gaol for his mother! That's what he'd come to tell you that night.'

Simon nodded. 'So it seems. Fool. He didn't get around to it and if he had I would have tried to talk him out of it. I'm not surprised he didn't rush into an explanation. He knew I would have told him that taking the blame for his mother wouldn't help her at all.'

What kind of man made that sort of sacrifice without flinching? Actually, her man. 'He went to prison for her. Lost his job and his reputation.' And me, she thought, but didn't say it. Well, he hadn't lost her yet.

Simon rubbed the back of his head. 'That news just makes me more angry with him. But I'll get over it.' He rubbed again. 'Obviously I'm still battling with the idea I didn't suspect Rayne would do that. Now it's glaringly obvious. So I let him down too.'

He put his finger up and pointed at her.

'Maybe you should do what he suggested. Lie down. You're as pale as a ghost and the family won't be here for another two hours for breakfast.'

Maybe she would. Because she had plans for tonight. 'I want Rayne to spend Christmas with us.'

Simon didn't look as surprised as she'd thought he would. He glanced at Tara and Maeve caught the almost imperceptible nod between them. 'Thought you might—just don't rush into anything,' was all he said.

Rayne threw his duffle bag on the floor of the sparse hotel room and himself onto the single bed on his back. He'd had to knock on the residence door to ask if they were opening today. The guy had said not officially and let him in. Given him a room and said he'd fix him up tomorrow.

Rayne pulled the packet of letters from his

pocket and eased open the first one. Started to read about Maeve's pregnancy. After ten minutes, and an aching, burning feeling in his gut, he loosened his belt and lay down on the bed. His mind expanded with images, good and bad, of his time with Maeve and what she'd gone through because he hadn't been there for her. He couldn't stomach it. He searched for something else to think about until he got over the pain.

He reached his hands arms up behind his head and sighed. One thing about prison, you lost your finicky ways about where you could sleep.

It was a typical country pub. With typical country hospitality, seeing he could be sleeping on a park bench if they hadn't let him in.

Squeaky cast-iron bedframe with yellowed porcelain decoration in the middle, thin, lumpy mattress, used-to-be white sheets and a wrinkled bedspread. A hook for clothes and a bathroom down the hall to share, except that no one else was such a loser they were in there for Christmas.

He wouldn't be here long. Wasn't sure he should be in Lyrebird Lake at all. But thank God he'd come.

Maeve was having his baby. Maeve, who was anything but 'little Princess Maeve'. How the hell had that happened when they'd been so careful?

Funnily, he didn't even consider it could be anyone else's because the dates matched and after what they had shared—Lord, what they had shared in one incredible night—if a persistent sperm was going to get through any night that would be the one. He half laughed out loud—a strangled, confused noise—thankful that nobody else would hear or care about it.

A ridiculous mix of horror that a child had been dumped with him for a parent, regret at how distressed Simon must have been at his supposed friend's perfidy, ghastly regret that

Maeve had had to face Simon without him and spend a pregnancy without his support.

But on top, like a life-raft shining light in the dark ocean, was an insidious, floating joy that glorious Maeve had kept his child and he was going to be a father. And she'd held his hand in front of Simon.

Though the next steps held a whole bag of dilemmas. What was he going to do about it? What could he do about it? Of course he would support them, money wasn't a problem. Hell, he'd buy her a house and put it in her name, or the baby's name, whatever she wanted. But what else?

Suddenly his whole world had changed, from that of a lost soul who hadn't been able to help his own mother—the one person he'd tried so hard to save—to a social pariah without any commitments and little motivation to slip back into his previous life, and now to a man with the greatest responsibility of all. Protecting another woman, keeping in mind he hadn't been able to save the last one, and this time his child as well, was something which scared him to the core.

Of course, that was if they could possibly work something out, and if she'd let him, but at least she wanted to talk. He wasn't so sure Simon wanted to and he really couldn't blame him.

It was a lot to take in. And a lot to lose when you thought you'd already lost it all.

Maeve saw Rayne arrive because she was standing at the window of her bedroom, waiting. It was nine-thirty and everyone had arrived for breakfast and the huge pile of family presents were to be opened after that.

She shook her head as the black car stopped, so antique it was trendy again, big and bulky and mean looking, very *James Dean, I'm a bad boy*, Rayne really needed to get over that image. Especially now he was going to be a father. She smiled ironically through the window. Though if Rayne had a son her child would probably love that car as he grew up.

She turned away from the window and glanced at the mirror across the room. So it seemed after only one sight of Rayne she was thinking of her child growing up with him.

She saw her reflection wincing back at her. The worried frown on her brow. Saw the shine reflected on her face and she crossed the room to re-powder her nose.

Was she doing the right thing, going with her feelings? she thought as she dabbed. Should she believe so gullibly that there might be a future with Rayne? Take it slowly, her brother had said. Maybe Simon was right.

She reapplied her lip gloss. At least she'd been the first point of call as soon as he was free, and that had been before he'd known she was having his baby.

Or was she having herself on. Maybe it was

Simon, his best friend from his childhood, not her he'd really come to see. He had travelled across the world last time for a conversation with Simon that hadn't happened. This morning he'd just seen her on the side of the road first.

When it all boiled down to it. how much did Rayne know about her or could care after just one night? One long night when they hadn't done much talking at all.

Nope. She wasn't a stand-out-in-the-crowd success story.

With a mother who expected perfection and three older, very confident sisters, she'd always wanted to shine in the crowd. Had hidden her shyness under a polished and bolshie exterior that had said, *Look at me*, had forced herself to be outgoing. Maybe that was why her relation-ships with men had seemed to end up in disaster.

Once they'd got to know her and realised she wasn't who they'd thought she was.

That was her problem. Being the youngest of five very successful siblings, she'd always seen herself falling a little short. But finally, when she'd settled on midwifery, incredibly she'd loved it. But her job had gone down the tube with this baby for a while yet—so she'd blown that too.

The hardest thing about Rayne walking away without a backward glance had been those voices in her head saying it had been easy for him to do that. Too easy.

She turned away from the mirror with a sigh. And then there was Rayne's consummate ease in keeping the whole impending disaster of his court appearance and sentencing from her.

But what if she had the chance to show him the real woman underneath? Maybe he'd show her the real man? Maybe it could work because there was no doubting physical chemistry was there in spades between them. Or had been before she'd turned into a balloon. They'd just have to see if that was enough to build on with their child.

She slid her hand gently over the mound of her stomach and held the weight briefly in her palm.

You are the most important person, baby, but maybe your daddy just needs to have someone with faith in him to be the perfect father. And I do have that faith and he'll have to prove otherwise before we are going to be walked away from again.

CHAPTER FOUR

Christmas Day

RAYNE PULLED UP outside the place Maeve had called the manse. The phone call had come sooner than he'd expected. Apparently he was down for family breakfast *and* lunch. He wasn't sure if could mentally do that but he'd see how it turned out.

As he gently closed the door of the car he glanced at motorised nodding animals in the Christmas manger on the lawn and shook his head. There was a little straw-filled crib with a tiny swaddled baby in it, and for a minute he thought it was a real baby; rubbed his eyes and, of course, it was a doll. He was seeing babies everywhere. Not surprising really.

But there were definite adoring looks and nods from the mechanical Mary and Joseph, and the three wise men and those crazy manger animals nodded along.

He could imagine during the weeks leading up to Christmas it wouldn't be unusual for children to drop by on the way home from school to check out the display.

He'd sort of noticed the display but not really when he'd been here earlier. He stopped for a moment and took in the full glory of the scene. Geez. Now, that was schmaltz with a capital S.

It was so over the top, with the solar mini-train circling the yard carrying fake presents, the fairy-lights all over the house and around the manger, and the giant blue star on the main building roof, totally the opposite of Maeve and Simon's mother's idea of colour-coordinated, understated elegance. Or his own poor mother's belief it was all a waste of time.

Imagine a family who was willing to put that much effort into decorations that only hung around for a month and then had to be packed away again. He couldn't help but speculate how much they'd be willing to put into things that were really important.

It was so hard to imagine that sort of close-knit caring. The kind he'd seen between Maeve and Simon's family every time he'd visited their house.

He'd always told Simon he was lucky, having two families and six sisters, and Simon had said he could share them as long as he didn't chat them up.

Well, that one had been blown out of the water with Maeve, he thought with a grimace, though he and Maeve hadn't done much chatting.

He sighed. Pulled back his shoulders and lifted his chin. Started to walk again. Not something to be proud of. Well, that's what he was here for. To make right what he could. Maeve had said they needed to talk but he wasn't so sure Simon was going to come to the party.

The front screen door opened and Simon met him as he came up the steps. And held out his hand. There was a definite welcome there he hadn't expected. Holy hell. Rayne's throat burned and he swallowed.

Simon shrugged and smiled. 'Can't say I've been happy but it is good to see you.' Then he stepped in and hugged him.

Rayne's choked throat felt like someone had shoved a carpenter's wood rasp down his neck, not that he'd ever cried, even when he'd buried his mother, so it was an unfamiliar and uncomfortable feeling, but he hadn't expected this. He gripped Simon's hand so hard his friend winced and he loosened his fingers. Dropped the handshake.

'Um. Thanks. That was unexpected.'

'I've had time to cool down. And I'm sorry about your mother.' A hard stare. 'You taking the blame for her is something we'll talk about another time.'

His throat still felt tight. He so hadn't expected this. 'Maeve is incredible.'

Simon snorted. 'Or incredibly stupid. We'll see which one.' He shrugged, definitely warmer than earlier that morning, and gestured to the door. 'Now come in. It's Christmas and you're about to meet the rest of the family. By the way, my dad knows all about you.' Simon raised his brows.

Raised his own back. 'Nice.' Not. Rayne glanced over his shoulder at the road but there was only his car on the street. He'd hoped as there were no other cars he could come and go before the family arrived.

Simon must have seen his look because he said, 'Everyone walks most places around here. They're all out the back.'

They walked through the house down a central hallway, past some mistletoe he needed to avoid unless Maeve was there, with at least three rooms each side, and into a large kitchen, heavily decorated for Christmas, complete with multi-coloured gifts under the tree. At the kitchen bench a tiny, round, older lady with a Santa hat on her white hair was carving ham slices onto a plate. The young blonde woman he'd seen earlier that morning was piling fried eggs onto another carving plate.

'This is Rayne, Louisa. My grandmother, Rayne.'

The older lady looked up and glowed at Simon and then with twinkling eyes skimmed Rayne from head to toe with apparent delight. 'Maeve's mystery man. You are very welcome, my dear. And just in time for breakfast. Merry Christmas.'

Just in time for breakfast? His stomach rumbled. He hadn't even thought about food. She was a jolly little thing and jolliness had been hard to come by lately. He couldn't help a small smile. 'Merry Christmas to you.'

Simon's voice warmed even more. 'And this divine being is my fiancée, Tara. Tara's a mid-wife at the birth centre and has been looking after Maeve's pregnancy since she arrived. If you're good, we might even invite you to our wedding.'

'Hello, Rayne. Welcome. Merry Christmas.' And Tara, a much younger small blonde woman with wise eyes, smiled a smile that said, *I know how hard it is for you at this moment*. And, incredibly, he actually believed her. Now, that was strange.

Tara handed him the heaped plate. 'Take this out with you when you go, could you, please, and try to find a spot on the table for it.'

He took the plate and she gestured Simon to a basket of rolls, which he obligingly picked up right after he'd kissed her swiftly on her mouth. She laughed and shooed him off and Rayne looked away. He couldn't ever imagine being so easy with Maeve.

There was a brief lull in the conversation when they opened the screen door out into the back yard, but Rayne had spotted Maeve and the voices were fading anyway as his eyes drank in the sight of her.

Damn, she looked amazing in a red summer dress, like a ripe plum, the material ballooned over her magnificent belly and shimmered when she shifted. A green Christmas scarf draped her gorgeous shoulders. She looked like his fantasy Mrs Santa Claus and he had to hold himself back as Simon introduced him to his other family.

A tall, powerfully built man crossed to them. He put his hand out to Rayne and he took it. Shook firmly and stepped back. Yep. That had to be Simon's natural father. Same mouth and nose. A chip off the old block, and he reminded him of an army major he'd know once. 'Pleased to meet you, sir.'

'Angus, not sir. And I understand you're a paediatrician?'

'Not for nearly a year.'

'Maybe we'll get a chance to talk about that while you're here. You could think of having a breather here while you settle back into some kind of routine.'

Not likely. He already wanted to run. 'Perhaps.'

A vivacious redhead swooped in and gave him a hug. He tried awkwardly to return it but he'd never been a hugger. Her head only came up to his chin. 'Merry Christmas, Rayne. I'm Simon's stepmother, Mia.'

She stepped back and waved to two young miniatures of herself at the table. 'And our daughters Amber and Layla. So there will be nine of us for breakfast.'

It felt like a lot more but, really, the only person he wanted to talk to there was Maeve, who was watching him with an enigmatic expression, and it looked like they'd have to eat before he'd get any chance of that.

Tara and Louisa brought the last two plates and they all began to sit at the long table under the tree, but as he crossed to Maeve she moved towards the table as if she felt more confident there. With definite intent he held her chair and then settled himself beside her.

He glanced around and hoped nobody could see he really didn't want to be here, then he pulled himself up. It was Christmas.

One of the little girls said grace, and he acknowledged the nice touch, especially as he would have been stumped if someone had asked him, and the table groaned with food. He hadn't seen this much food since that Christmas at Simon's all those years ago.

When grace was over he turned to Maeve.

She was why he was here. Funny how Simon had slipped back into second place, though it was good to see him too. His only friend in the world, and he'd thought he'd lost him.

But Maeve. She looked even better up close. Much more colour in her cheeks than earlier. He lowered his voice because he imagined she wouldn't want to draw attention to the fact she'd fainted that morning. 'Are you okay?'

A brief glimpse of her confusion as she looked at him. 'I'm fine.'

'Fine as in Freaked Out, Insecure, Neurotic and Emotional?' He tried a poor attempt at a joke.

A longer look. 'They been showing you movies in there?'

He felt his face freeze. His body go cold with the memories. 'No.'

Then he saw the distress that filled her eyes and her hand came across and touched his. Stayed for a second, warmed him like an injection of heat up his arm, and then shifted back to her lap. 'I'm sorry. It was a stupid joke.'

'Ditto. From another movie.' He forced a smile. 'It's fine.'

Her face softened. 'You sure? You know what "fine" means?'

He so didn't want to play, even though he'd started it. 'How long do we have to stay? I need to talk to you.'

She glanced around to make sure nobody had heard. It wasn't a problem because everyone was talking and laughing full steam ahead and the little girls were bouncing in their seats. Maeve's eyes softened when she looked at them. 'Until after the presents, and then I don't have to be back here until this afternoon.'

'So you'll come with me for a couple of hours. Talk in private? Sort what we can?'

He felt her assessing look. 'We can do that. Not sure how much we can sort in a couple of hours. As long as you get me back here before

Christmas lunch at three o'clock. I promised to make the brandy sauce.' She glanced under her brows at him. 'I can cook when I feel like it, you know.'

'Oh. I know.'

It was all still there. Maeve could feel the vibration of chemistry between them. Just an inch or two between her skin touching his skin and even then his heat was radiating into her shoulder in waves without the contact. And all this at the Christmas breakfast table in front of Simon's family.

How could this man make her so aware of every part of her body, and why him? He curled her toes, made her nipples peak, her belly twist and jump, and that was without the baby doing its own gyrations in there. It was darned awkward and the only consolation was he didn't look any more comfortable than she was.

But this was way more important than incredible sex. This was about the future, and even she had to admit she hadn't given the future a thought last time they'd been together. He'd been pretty adamant there hadn't been a future if she remembered rightly, though she had expected a little more pillow talk the next day rather than him being marched away by federal police.

She caught Tara's concerned eyes on her and shrugged. She'd be okay. Early days yet. But to think that this morning she'd been crying into her pillow, wanting him to be here for the birth, and here he was within an inch of her. It was a lot to take in. And she couldn't help the tiny beam of light that suggested she'd been given a blessing to be thankful for.

Someone asked her to pass a plate of tomatoes. There was a lot of eating going on all around them and she and Rayne hadn't started yet. Maybe they'd better.

Rayne must have thought the same because he

passed her the ham and she took a small piece, glanced at his plate, and saw at least he was preparing to be fed. Then he passed her the eggs and she took one of those as well. Though she didn't feel like putting anything into her mouth. Her belly was squirming too much.

People were putting their knives and forks together and sitting back. Leaning forward again and pouring coffee and juice. Maeve reached over and brought the rolls over in front of her, gave one to Rayne and one to herself without thinking and then realised she was acting like an old housewife looking after her husband.

He lifted his brows and smiled sardonically at her and she shrugged. 'Enjoy.' Reminded herself that she'd been a confident woman the last time he'd seen her and she needed to keep that persona even more now she was fighting for her baby's future. But what if she wasn't enough? What if he still left after their talk today? Surely he wouldn't leave this afternoon after just getting here.

'How long can you stay around here?'

He paused with his fork halfway to his mouth. Good timing at least. 'When is the baby due?'

'Tomorrow.'

His face paled and she thought, *Tell me about it, buster, I'm the one who has to do it.* 'But I expect I'll go overdue. Does it matter what date?'

He shook his head, clearly rattled by the impending birth. Put his fork down. Couldn't he see her belly looked like it was about to explode?

Then he said quietly, aware that a few ears were straining their way, 'I have no commitments, if that's what you mean.'

She sniffed at that. 'You do now.'

He glanced around the table. Saw Simon and his father watching them. 'I'll be here for as long as you want me to be here. It's the least I can do.'

If only he hadn't added that last sentence. The relief she'd felt hearing him say he'd stay as long as she needed him was lost with the tone of sacrifice. Before she could comment, and it would have been unwise whatever she'd been going to say, at the very least, he touched her hand.

'Sorry. That came out wrong. It's just that I'm still getting used to you expecting a baby. And this table is killing me.'

Just then Mia stood up. 'The girls want to know how long before everyone is finished.'

Maeve pushed her plate away thankfully. 'I'm done.'

Rayne stood up. 'Let me help clear.' And he began very efficiently scraping and collecting plates, and she remembered him rinsing his plate at Simon's house.

At least he was house-trained, she thought with an internal smile as she began to gather up side plates, probably a lot more than she was. It was a warming thought that maybe there was stuff that they could do for each other, maybe there were things they could share between them that they'd find out and enjoy as well.

Within a very short time the dishwasher was loaded, the leftovers were stowed in the fridge and the kitchen clean. The big sunroom area of the back room at the end of the kitchen had been cleared when the kitchen table had gone outside and the Christmas tree was surrounded by lots of presents, as well as chairs and cushions so everyone had a niche to perch to watch the fun.

Simon had Tara on his lap, Mia and Angus were sitting with Louisa on the lounge they'd pulled in, and the girls were hopping and crawling around the tree as they shared out the presents one at a time.

Everyone sat except Rayne. He leant against the wall to the left of Maeve so he could watch her face, and he knew she wished he'd take the chair Simon had offered and sit down next to her. But he didn't. He didn't deserve to be a part of the circle. Felt more of an outsider than he ever had, despite the efforts of others. It was his fault he felt like that and he knew it. Just couldn't do anything about it.

He watched Simon take a present from the eldest child and hand it solemnly to Tara. When she opened it he saw her eyes flash to Simon's, saw the tremulous smile and the stroke of her finger down the painted face of the Russian doll. Those dolls that had other dolls inside. This looked like a very expensive version of those.

Cute. But a strange present to give. Though he had no idea about giving presents himself. He frowned, realising he should have thought about that on the way here. He didn't have any to give.

Tara didn't seem to know about the tinier dolls inside and Simon laughed and showed her how they came apart and another pretty painted doll was removed from the centre. And another and another. Until there was a dozen little painted dolls in a line along the arm of the chair. Simon's little sisters had eyes wide with wonder and he suspected there was a little moisture in Tara's eyes, and even Maeve's. He was missing something here.

Maeve shifted her body so she was closer to him and gestured for him to lean down.

'Tara's parents died when she was six. So she was in an orphanage until she grew up. Since then she's never owned a doll.'

Damn! No wonder she understood a little of his awkwardness on arrival. He wasn't the only one who'd had it hard. He'd always been grateful his mum had stayed straight long enough to keep him out of care. Even though he'd been the one doing the caring at home. At least it had been his home and he had had a mother.

The present-giving moved on and Maeve was given a little hand-made wheatpack, a drink bottle with a straw, and a pair of warm socks as comfort aids for labour, and they all laughed.

He watched Maeve smile and thank Tara, but the little twitch in her eyelid made him wonder just how calm the woman having his baby really was about the approaching birth.

His own uneasiness grew with the thought. It wasn't like neither of them didn't know a lot about birth. He'd been at many, but mostly he had been the paediatrician there for Caesarean babies or other newborns at risk.

And Maeve had done her midwifery so she was well versed in what would happen. But it was a bit different when it was this close to home. There were those other times when the unexpected happened.

He really needed to talk to her about that. He glanced at the clock. Fifteen minutes since last time he'd looked at it. Not too bad. And then it was over. The paper was collected, hugs were exchanged and everyone sat back. Louisa asked about fresh coffee or tea and Maeve shifted to the edge of her chair. He put out his hand and helped her up.

Her hand felt good in his. He tightened his grip.

'We're going for a drive.' She said it to the room in general and there was a little pause in the conversation. Then she looked at Louisa and smiled. 'I'll be back by two-thirty to make that brandy sauce.'

Simon groaned. 'Make sure you are. That sauce is to die for.' Everyone laughed again and Rayne wondered, with dry amusement, if he really was the only one who got the warning directed their way.

Louisa said, 'Hold on for a minute.'

And Maeve shrugged and said, 'I'll just go to the loo before we go.' He thought they'd never get away.

Then Louisa was back with a small basket. Quickest pack he'd ever seen. 'Just a Thermos of tea and a cold drink. Some Christmas cake and rum balls in case you get hungry.'

He looked at her. 'I'm pretty sure nobody could be hungry leaving this house.' Looked at her plump cheeks, pink from exertion. Her kind eyes crinkled with the pleasure of giving her food. 'Thank you.' He lowered his voice so that nobody else heard. 'I was going to take Maeve to the seats by the boatshed. This is perfect.'

She held up a finger. 'One more thing, then.' And within seconds was back with a small brown paper bag. 'Bread scraps for the ducks.'

He shook his head. He had never ever met anyone like her. 'You are my new favourite person.'

Then Maeve came back and he tucked the paper bag into his pocket so he could take her hand and carried the basket in the other.

CHAPTER FIVE

The lake

DRIVING AWAY FROM the house, he felt like a load fell from his shoulders. He never had done other people's family events well and the feeling of being an outcast had grown exponentially when he'd had to add the words 'ex-inmate' to his CV.

He realised Maeve was quiet too, not something he remembered about her, and he looked away from the road to see her face. Beautiful. She was watching him. He looked back at the road. Better not run over any kids on Christmas morning, riding their new bikes.

'So where are we going?'

'I saw a boathouse down on the lake. Thought

we'd just sit on one of the park benches beside
the water.' He looked at her again. 'That okay?'
He could smell the scent of her hair from where
he was sitting. He remembered that citrus smell
from nine months ago.

'Sure.' She shrugged and glanced at the seat
between them. 'What's in the basket?'

He had to smile at that. Smile at the memory
of Louisa's need to give. 'Emergency food sup-
plies Simon's grandmother worried we might
need.'

Maeve peered under the lid and groaned. 'She
put in rum balls. I love rum balls. And I can't
have them.'

He frowned. She could have what she liked.
He'd give her the world if he had the right. 'Why
can't you have rum balls?'

She sighed with exasperation. 'Because I'm
pregnant and foetuses don't drink alcohol.'

He looked at her face and for the first time in

a long time he felt like laughing. But he wasn't sure he'd be game to.

Instead, he said, trying to keep his mouth serious, 'I hope our baby appreciates the sacrifices its mother has been through.'

Tartly. 'I hope its father does.'

That was a kick to the gut. He did. Very much. He turned into the parking area of the boatshed and parked. Turned off the engine. Turned to face her.

'Yes. I do. And I am sorry I haven't been here for you.'

She sighed. 'I'm sorry you didn't know. That I couldn't share the pregnancy with you.'

He thought of his state of mind in that prison if he'd known Maeve was pregnant and he couldn't get to her. God, no. 'I'm not.' He saw her flinch.

'Surely you don't mean that now. That's horrible.' She opened the car door and he could feel her agitation. Regretted immensely he'd hurt her, but couldn't regret the words. Saw her struggle to get out of the low car with her centre of balance all haywire from the awkwardness of the belly poking out front.

Suddenly realised it sounded harsh from her perspective. He didn't know how to explain about the absolute hell of being locked up. About the prospect of staying locked up for years. About his guilt that his mother had died to get him out and he'd actually been glad. He still couldn't think about the load of guilt that carried. He opened his own door and walked swiftly round to help her out.

Finally Rayne said very quietly, 'I would have gone mad if I'd known you were pregnant and I couldn't get to you. There was a chance I wasn't coming out for years and years.'

She stopped struggling to get herself from the car. Wiped the tears on her cheek. Looked up at him. 'Oh. Is that why you didn't read the letters?'

'I lost access to everything, Maeve. I was a faceless perpetrator surrounded by men who hated the world. I'd never hated the world before but I hated it in there. The only way I could stay sane in that toxic environment was to seal myself off from it. Create a wall and not let anything in. The last thing I needed was sunshine that I couldn't touch and that's what your letters were to me. That way led to madness and I had to stay strong behind my wall.'

'I shouldn't have sent them, then?'

It certainly hadn't been her fault for sending them. She was an angel—especially now he'd read them. 'You couldn't have known. But they were something I looked forward to. I was going to open them when I got out. As soon as I got out. But then I got scared you would tell me not to come and I needed to see you and Simon one more time to explain. So I decided to open them after I saw you.' He rubbed the back of his neck. 'I'm so sorry I caused you pain.'

* * *

Maeve looked up at Rayne and saw what she'd seen nine months ago. Big shoulders under a black shirt, black hair cut shorter to the strong bones of his head, dark, dark eyes, even more difficult to read, but maybe they were only easy to read on the way to the bedroom. And that wicked mouth, lips that could work magic or drop words that made her go cold.

This was going to be tougher than she'd expected it to be. Something Tara had said to her a couple of days ago filtered back into her memory. Something about her knowing men who had been to prison and were harder, more distanced from others when they got out.

The problem was Rayne had already been distanced from people before he'd been wrongly convicted.

But when he'd said he was glad he hadn't opened her letters, and she'd responded emotionally with the hurt of it, she'd been thinking about herself. Not about why he would say something hurtful like that. Not about what he'd been through. She promised herself she would try to help heal the scars that experience had left him with—not make the whole transition more difficult.

Guess she'd have to learn to filter her reactions through his eyes. And that wasn't going to be easy because she liked looking at things her way.

But it should be easier with him here, not harder. The thought made her feel cross. 'For goodness' sake, help me out of this damn car.' Not what she'd intended to say but now she thought about it she'd be a whole lot more comfortable with him not standing over her.

The dirty rat laughed.

But at least he put his hand out and again she sailed upwards with ridiculous ease until she was standing beside him.

'You really are a princess, you know that?'

She glared at him as she adjusted her dress and straightened her shoulders. Re-establishing her personal space. 'You have a problem with that?'

He looked at her, and if she wasn't mistaken there could even be a little softening in that hard expression. 'Nope. I love it.'

Warmth expanded inside her. There was hope for the man yet.

Rayne shut the door behind her and picked up the basket. Tucked her hand under his other arm, and she liked that closeness as they sauntered across to the lakeside seats.

Like nothing was wrong. She let it go. She'd always been a 'temper fast and then forget it' person so that was lucky because she had the feeling they had a bit of getting used to each other to come.

Further down the shore, a young boy and his dad were launching an obviously new sailing boat into the lake and a small dog was barking at the ducks heading their way away from those other noisy intruders.

'I love ducks,' Maeve said. 'Always have. I used to have a baby one, it grew up to be an amazing pet. Used to waddle up and meet me when I came home from school.'

'What did you call it?'

She could feel a blush on her cheeks. He was going to laugh. Maybe she could make up a different name. A cool one.

He bumped her shoulder gently with his as if he'd read her mind. 'I want the real name.'

She glared at him. 'I was going to give you the real one.'

'Sure you were.'

Quietly. 'Cinderella.'

Yep, he laughed. But it was a good sound. And so did she. Especially for Christmas morning, from a man only a few weeks out of prison who'd recently lost his mother and found out he was going to be a father. Going to be a father very soon. It felt good she'd made him laugh.

'Imagine,' he said. Then he turned and studied her face. His eyes were unreadable but his voice was sombre. 'Thank you for even thinking of giving me a chance.' And when she saw the sincerity, and just a touch of trepidation, now she felt like crying.

Wasn't sure she should tell him about this morning—what if she scared him?—but couldn't resist the chance. 'You know, I woke up today and all I wanted for Christmas was to be able to talk to you.'

His eyes widened in shock. And something else—she wasn't sure but it could have been fear. Yep, she'd scared him. Fool.

She felt her anger rise. Anger because it shouldn't be this hard to connect with a guy she'd been powerless to resist and it wasn't like he'd been doing something he hadn't agreed to either that night they'd created this baby together. So there was a force greater than them that she believed in but she wasn't so sure it worked if only one of them was a convert. 'It's not that hard to understand. I'm having a baby and there is supposed to be two of us. And if you don't hate me, think about it.'

She turned away from him. Didn't want to see anything negative at this moment. She watched the little boy jumping up and down as his little sailing boat picked up the breeze and sailed out towards the middle of the lake.

Nope. She needed to say it all. Get it out there because if it wasn't going to happen she needed to know now. She turned back to him. 'So what I'm saying is thank you for coming, even though you didn't know I was pregnant, thank you for driving all this way on Christmas to see us.'

'That's nothing.'

'I haven't finished.'

He held up his hands. 'Go on, then.'

'If you want to do the right thing, do something for me.' She took a big breath. 'I'm asking you to stay. At least until after the birth. Be with me during the birth, because if you're there I will be able to look forward to this occasion as I should be—not dreading the emptiness and fear of being alone.'

Rayne got that. He also got how freaking brave this woman was. To lay herself out there to be knocked back—not that he would, but, sheesh, how much guts had it taken for her to actually put that request into words? He felt the rock in his heart that had cracked that morning shift and crack a little more.

Heck. 'Of course I'll stay. Just ask for anything.' Well, not anything. He didn't think he was the type of guy to move in with, play happy families with, but he could certainly see himself being a little involved with the baby. He was good with babies. Good with children. For the first time in a long time he remembered he had an amazing job helping children and their parents and maybe it was a job he should go back to some time.

But he had no experience about making a family. No idea how to be a father. No idea what a father even did, except for those he'd seen at work. Simon's father had just seemed to be 'there'. He didn't know how to do 'being there'.

He glanced around the peaceful scene. Another little family were riding shiny pushbikes along the path. They all wore matching red helmets. The dad was riding at the back and he guessed he was making sure everyone was okay. That seemed reasonable. Maybe he could do that. The birds were chirping and hopping in the branches above his head like the thoughts in his brain.

This place had an amazing vibe to it. Or it could be the collective consciousness of celebrating Christmas with family and friends creating the goodwill. But he'd never felt anything like it. He looked at Maeve. Or seen anyone like her.

She was staring over the water into the distance but there was tension in her shoulders. Rigidity in her neck. And he'd put that there. He'd need to be a lot better at looking after her if he was going to be her support person in one of the most defining moments of her life. Of both their lives.

He stepped up behind her and pulled her back to lean into his body. Lifted his hands to her shoulders and dug gently into the firm muscles, kneaded with slowly increasing depth until she moaned and pushed her bottom back into him until her whole weight was sagged against him.

She moaned again and he could feel the stir of his body as it came awake. Down, boy. Not now. Definitely not now. He could barely get his head around any of this, let alone lose the lot in a fog of Maeve sex.

'That feels *so-o-o* good,' she said.

He just knew her eyes were closed. He smiled. 'I'd need to get lots of practice to build up my stamina for the event.'

'Mmm-hmm,' she agreed sleepily.

He shifted his fingers so that they were circling the hard little knot in her neck and she drooped even more.

'You might need to sit down.' He could hear the smile in his voice. Drew her to the bench they were standing beside and steered her into a sitting position. Went back around the bench so he was standing behind her—which helped the libido problem as he wasn't touching her whole body now.

He began again. Slow circular rotations of his fingers, kneading and swirling and soothing the rigidity away, for her, anyway. His body was as stiff as a pole.

He'd never had this desire to comfort and heal a woman before. Plenty of times he'd wanted to carry one to bed with him, but this? This was different. His hand stilled.

'Don't stop.'

He stepped back. Created distance from something he knew he wasn't ready for. Might never be ready for. 'I remembered the bread.' Pulled the brown paper bag from his pocket and gave it to her. A heaven-sent distraction to stop her interrogation into why he'd stepped back.

'For the ducks,' he said.

'Oh.' He heard the disappointment fade from her voice. Watched her straighten her shoulders with new enthusiasm. She was like a child. And he envied her so much. He couldn't remember when he'd felt like a child.

Then she was into planning mode again. 'You'll have to stay at the manse so I can find you when I need you.'

Just like that. Room, please. 'I can't just gate-crash Simon's grandmother's house.'

She threw a knobby crust of bread at a duck,

which wrestled with it in a splash of lake water. 'Sure you can. Locum doctors and agency midwives come all the time when one of the hospital staff goes away. That's where they stay. The manse has lots of rooms and Louisa loves looking after people.'

Unfortunately too easy. He'd said he'd be there for the birth. He said he'd be her support person. He'd said he'd do anything and the second thing she asked for he was thinking, No!

H pushed back the panic. It would be better than the hotel. And not as bad as just moving into a house with Maeve and having her there twenty-four seven as his responsibility not to let anything happen to her.

Now, that was a frightening thought.

He wasn't on a good statistical run with saving people, which would be why he was an orphan now, and he went cold. Couldn't imagine surviving if anything happened to Maeve on his watch.

He did not want to do this. 'Sure. If Simon's grandmother says it's fine.' He thought about his friend. 'If Simon doesn't think I'm pushing my way into his family.'

'Simon spends every available minute with Tara. Which reminds me. Tara is my midwife. I might ask her to run through some stuff with us for working together in labour. She's done a course and it works beautifully for couples.'

His neck tightened and he resisted the impulse to rub it. Hard. Or turn and run away. Couple? Now they were a couple? She must have sensed his withdrawal because she made a little sound of distress and he threw her a glance. Saw a pink flood of colour rise from her cleavage. Was distracted for a moment at the truly glorious sight that was Meave's cleavage, and then looked up at her face.

She mumbled, 'I meant a couple as in you are my support person in labour.'

Hell. He nodded, dropped his hands back onto

her shoulders. Tried not to glance over the top of her so he could see down her dress. He was an emotionally stunted disgrace, and he had no idea what Maeve saw in him or why she would want to continue seeing him. He needed to be thankful she was willing to include him at all.

But he couldn't come up with any words to fix it. He watched her throw some more bread scraps to a flotilla of black ducks that had made an armada towards Maeve. They were floating back and forth, their little propeller legs going nineteen to the dozen under the water. A bit like he was feeling, with all these currents pulling him every which way.

Across the lake the Christmas sailboat was almost at the other side. He could see the father and the little boat boy walking around the path to meet it. That father knew what to do. He wasn't stressing to the max about letting his kid down. What training did he have? Maybe, if bad things didn't happen, if he didn't stuff up, if Maeve didn't realise she deserved way better than him, he'd do that one day with his own son.

Or kick a ball. Ride bikes with him and buy him a little red helmet.

Or maybe Maeve's baby would be a little miniature Maeve. That was really scary. Imagine having to keep her safe? The air around him seemed to have less oxygen that it had before, leaving him with a breathless feeling.

'Want to see what's in the basket?' Maeve was pulling it onto the seat beside her. 'We'd better eat something out of it before we go back.'

She handed him the rum balls. 'Eat these so I don't.' Began to put mugs and spoons out.

He took them. Battened down the surge of responsibility that was crowding in on him as Maeve began to make a little picnic. Like any other family at the side of the lake. He didn't know where the conversation should go or what he was supposed to do. She handed him a cup of tea and he almost dropped it.

He felt her eyes on him. 'Relax, Rayne.' Her voice was soft, understanding, and he wasn't sure he deserved that understanding but he did allow his shoulders to drop a little. 'It's all been a shock for you. Let's get through the next week and worry about long term later. I'm just glad you're here and that you've said you'll stay for the labour.'

She was right. He felt the stress leach away like the tea seemed to have soaked into the brown dirt. He sat down beside her.

She handed him the bag of crumbs. 'Bread-throwing is therapeutic.'

Like a child. 'You are therapeutic.' But he took the bag. Before he could throw more crumbs, a tiny, yapping black-curled poodle came bounding up to them, the red bow around his neck waving in the slight breeze. He raced at the ducks and stopped at the edge of the water, and the black ducks took off in a noisy burst of com-

plaint because they'd just found another bene-
factor in Rayne and now they had to leave.

A little girl's tremulous cry called the dog
from further down the street and the black dog
turned, cocked an ear, and then bounded off towards his mistress.

'So much for duck therapy.'

'Poor Rayne. Come, snuggle up to me and I'll
make you feel better.'

He smiled and was about to say something
when they heard the quack of another duck
from the bushes beside them. He frowned and
they both looked.

'Is it a nest?'

'Could be tangled in something.' He was
about to stand up and check the bush when
the sound came again and the branches rustled
with movement. He stilled in case he fright-
ened whatever was caught in there and they
watched the bushes part until a little brown bird
appeared, not a duck at all, a slim bird with a

long drooping tail that shook itself free of the undergrowth.

'Ohh…' Maeve whispered on a long sigh of delight. 'It's not a duck making that noise—it's a lyrebird.'

Rayne watched in amazement. 'A lyrebird mimic? As in Lyrebird Lake? I guess that figures.' But there was something so amazing about the pure fearlessness of a wild creature glaring at them as it moved a step closer and cocked his head to stare their way.

Then the little bird, no larger than a thin hen, straightened, spread his fan-shaped tail in a shimmer of movement and proceeded to dance at the edge of the lake for Maeve and Rayne.

A gift for Christmas.

Backward and forward, shimmering his harp-shaped tail as it swayed above his feathered head, and Rayne had never seen anything like it in his life as he clutched Maeve's hand in his and felt the tight knot in his chest mysteriously loosen the longer it went on. He glanced at Maeve and saw silver tears glistening.

He hugged her closer, drank in the magic without questioning why they were being gifted with it. All too soon it was over and the tail was lowered. One more stern look from the bird and he stepped nonchalantly back into the bush and with a crackle of foliage he disappeared.

They didn't speak for a moment as the moment sank into both of them.

'Wow,' whispered Maeve.

'Wow is right,' Rayne said, as he turned and wiped away the silver droplets from Maeve's face. Leant over and kissed her damp cheek. 'I feel like we've just been blessed.'

'Me, too.' And they sat there in silence for a few minutes longer, in an aura of peace between them that had been missing before, and slowly the real ducks came floating back.

CHAPTER SIX

Back at the manse

WHEN THEY GOT back Maeve disappeared into the kitchen to make her brandy sauce. Most of the family were out in the back yard—apparently the Christmas lunch table was set out there again—and the little girls were engrossed in their new possessions.

Simon waylaid Rayne and steered him back out the door away from the family. 'So what have you two decided?'

Rayne wasn't sure he'd decided anything. Maeve had done all the planning and now it was up to him to keep his end of the bargain. 'Maeve wants me to stay for the birth. I've said I will.' Simon looked mildly pleased. 'It's the least I can do.' There was that statement that had upset Maeve and it didn't do anything positive to Simon's frame of mind either if the frown across his friend's brow was an indication. He had no idea why it kept popping out.

'Is it that hard to commit to that? You slept with her.' His friend was shaking his head.

He held up his hand. 'Simon, I'm sorry. The last time I saw you it was an awful night. My world was about to implode. I didn't intend to end up in bed with Maeve.' He paused. Looked back in his mind and shook his head. 'But you should have seen her. She was like some peach vision and she poleaxed me.'

Simon glanced sardonically at him. 'And she dragged you off to bed?'

'Nope.' He had to smile at that memory. 'I carried her.' And she'd loved it.

Simon raised his brows. 'Up two flights of stairs?' Then he put his hand up. 'Forget I asked that. Tara says the sparks from you two light up the room. I get that. I get being irresistibly drawn to someone. And I get that you don't do commitment.'

Simon laughed dryly. 'But I thought I didn't do commitment until my Tara came along.'

Rayne looked at his friend's face. Had never seen it so joyous. As if Simon had finally found his feet and the whole world. Rayne couldn't imagine that. 'I meant to say congratulations. Tara seems a wonderful woman.'

Simon's smile grew. 'She is. And she so tough and...' He stopped, shook his head ruefully. 'Nice diversion. But this is about you.' Simon searched his face and he flinched a little under the scrutiny. 'Are you in for the long haul?'

Freaking long haul. Geez. He didn't know if he would last a week. 'I'm in for the labour. I'm in for what I can do to help Maeve for the birth. But as soon as I cause problems in her life I'm out of here.'

'And if you don't cause problems in her life?'

The inference was he had already let her down, and he guessed he had.

'I didn't know she was pregnant.' Thank God.

Simon shrugged. 'Tara said you didn't open the mail. And I know you wouldn't answer my calls. Why?'

It was his turn to shrug but his bitterness swelled despite his effort to control it. 'I didn't want to bring her into that place. Either of you. I had to keep the good things pure. And when I got out, I didn't want to read that she might refuse to see me. So I came here first.'

'Have you read the letters now?'

'Yes.' Could feel the long stare from Simon. Those letters just reiterated how much he was capable of stuffing up other people's lives.

Simon sighed long and heavily. 'I love you, man. I'm even getting used to the idea that you will be in Maeve's life now. In all our lives. But don't stuff this up.'

So he'd read his mind? Rayne almost laughed,

even though it was far from funny. 'That's the friend I remember.'

'Yeah. Merry Christmas.' Simon punched his shoulder. 'Let's go ask Louisa if you can stay. She'll be over the moon. She likes you.'

'I get the feeling your grandmother likes everyone.'

Simon laughed. 'Pretty much.'

Maeve had already asked Louisa.

'Of course he can stay,' Louisa enthused. 'So he'll be with you when you have the baby.' She sighed happily. 'Things have a way of working out.'

Maeve grimaced on the inside. *Things weren't 'working out' yet.*

There were a lot of things she and Rayne had to sort yet, not the least his attitude of *It's the least I can do. Grrr.* But, she reminded herself, this morning she'd been on her own. And he was here!

The magnitude of that overwhelmed her for a moment and she paused in the rhythmic stirring of thickening liquid in the bowl and just soaked that in. Rayne was here. And he was staying. At least until after the birth, and that was all she could ask for. Yet! She wondered if they would actually get much alone time.

Wondered if he was up for that. Wished she was skinny and gorgeous and could drag him off to bed. Or be carried there by her gorgeous sex object 'partner', round belly and all.

Partner. She'd always been uncomfortable with that sterile word. Not that Rayne was obviously sterile. And he wasn't her boyfriend. He certainly wasn't her lover.

'You want me to do that?' Louisa's worried voice. Maeve jumped and stirred again in the nick of time before she made lumps in the sauce.

'Wool-gathering.' Louisa's favourite saying and she'd picked it up. It described her state of mind perfectly. Little floating fibres of thought creating a mess of tangles in her brain. Mushing together to make a ball of confused emotions and wishes and fears and silly impossible dreams. Like the flotsam of leftover wool collected from the bushes where the sheep had walked past.

Well, Rayne was nobody's sheep. He'd never been a part of the flock, had never followed the rules of society except when he'd taken his incredibly intelligent brain to med school at Simon's insistence.

Men's voices drifted their way.

And here they came. Simon and Rayne. Two men she loved. The thought froze the smile on her face. She really loved Rayne. Did she? Fancied him, oh, yeah. The guy could light her fire from fifty paces away. But love?

Maybe brotherly love. She looked at her brother, smiling at something Louisa had said. Nope. She didn't feel the way she felt about

Simon. And there was another bonus. She could stop fighting with Simon now that Rayne was back. Fait accompli.

Her mind eased back into the previous thought. The scary one. That she did really love Rayne. There was no 'might' about it. She really was in no better spot than she had been this morning because though Rayne was physically here she wasn't stupid enough to think he was in love with her. And he could leave and have any woman he wanted any time he wanted.

The sauce was ready and she poured it into the jug. The beauty of this recipe, the reason she was the only one who made it in her family, was the secret ingredient that stopped the film forming on the top. So it didn't grow a skin.

That was a joke. She needed the opposite. She needed to grow ten skins so she could quietly peel away a new layer of herself to show Rayne so that she didn't dump it all on him at once. Because she knew it would require patience if she wanted to help him see he had a chance of a future he'd never dreamed about.

That he could be the kind of man any child would be proud to call his or her father. The kind of man any woman wanted to share her full life with—not just the bedroom.

What was with these pregnancy hormones? She needed to stop thinking about the bedroom. She ran her finger down the spoon handle on the way to the sink. Coated her finger in the rich golden sauce. Lifted it to her lips and closed her eyes. Mmm…

Rayne tried not to stare at Maeve as she parted her lips to admit a custard-covered fingertip. Watched her savour the thick swirl. Shut her eyes. Sigh blissfully as she put the spoon in the sink. Geez. Give a guy a break. If the day hadn't been enough without the almost overwhelming urge to pick her up from amidst all these people and ravish a heavily pregnant woman.

Louisa was talking to him. 'Sorry.' He blinked and turned to the little woman and he had the idea she wasn't blind to what had distracted him if the twinkle in her eyes was anything to go by.

'I said if you would like to follow me I'll show you your room. It's small but I think you'll like the position. And all the rooms open out onto a veranda and have their own chair and table setting outside the door.' She bustled out of the kitchen and he followed.

'That's the bathroom. It's shared with Maeve and Simon and Tara.'

He nodded and paid a bit more attention to the fact that this old country manse had to be at least a hundred years old. The ceilings were a good twelve feet high and the wood-panelled walls looked solid and well built.

Louisa gestured to a door. 'Maeve said she didn't mind there was a connecting door between the two. Do you?' She twinkled up at him.

'Um. No. That will be fine.'

'I thought it might be. Especially as she's getting near to her time and if she wanted to she could leave the door open between you.'

It was a good idea. That look of nervous anticipation he'd seen in Maeve's eyes this morning, he didn't like to call it fear, did need addressing. And it wasn't like he hadn't seen her without clothes. He brought his mind sternly back to the present.

If he could help by being close then that would give him purpose as he tried to come to grips with becoming an unexpected part of a large, noisy, hugging family—all that contact took a bit of getting used to.

He still couldn't believe they weren't all wishing him back to prison away from Maeve. But he knew for a fact Maeve was glad to see him. Maybe too glad, considering the prize she'd won.

Louisa opened the door next to Maeve's and, sure enough, it was a small room, but it did have a double bed against the wall and a chest of drawers. All he needed. 'Thanks, Louisa. It's great. Can I fix you up for it?'

'Lordy, no. I don't need money. I'm well looked after. But you may end up working every now and then for Angus at the hospital if he gets stuck. Everyone helps everyone in Lyrebird Lake.'

Well, not where he'd come from. He felt like he'd fallen into some religious sect and they were going to ask for his soul soon, except he knew that Simon was regular. And Maeve. And this sweet, generous older lady was obviously sincere. So it looked like he had a casual job as well as a place to lay his head. Though he couldn't see him being needed much at the hospital. 'Maybe I can help around the house. Or the garden? I wouldn't say no to be able to burn off some energy.'

She looked at him, a good once-over that had him wishing he'd tucked his shirt in and shaved, but she nodded. 'I have a pile of wood I need chopped before winter. The axe is in the wee shed under the tank stand. It's a bit early in the year but whenever you feel the need you just go right ahead and chop.'

He grinned. Couldn't help himself. Of all the things he'd thought might happen as he'd driven through the night to get here, getting a job as a woodcutter hadn't figured in the speculations.

He followed her out. 'Have I got time to nip back to the pub and let them know I won't be staying?'

'Have you left anything there?'

'No.' You didn't leave things in pub accommodation. Or maybe you did in Lyrebird Lake. Who knew?

'Well, that's fine. Denny Webb will be over visiting his wife at the hospital. Angus will pass the message on to the ward sister.'

Louisa waved to his car out in the street. 'You could bring your things in and then wash in the bathroom if you want.' She had noticed the bristles. 'And we'll see you back in a few minutes because it's nearly time for Christmas lunch.'

Obediently Rayne walked out to his car and brought in his overnight bag. The rest of his stuff—one small suitcase—was under the tarpaulin in the back of the truck. Not that he had much. He'd pretty well given everything else away. Had never been one for possessions. Wasn't quite sure what had influenced him to buy the old Chev. He'd passed it in a car yard on his way in from the airport and it had reminded him of his mother in happier times.

After his sleep in the motel for eight hours he'd walked back to the car yard an hour before closing time. Had told the guy if he could arrange a full mechanical check by a third party, transfers and insurance and tank of petrol in the time they had left, he'd pay the full price.

By the time he'd had a feed and returned, his

car was waiting for him. So he did have one possession.

And an exit strategy. Both good things.

Walking back through the kitchen and outside, it seemed that Christmas lunch would be even noisier than breakfast.

Simon offered him a beer before they all sat down and, to hell with it, he took the glass and it was icy cold, and even though they were in the shade from the trees, it was pretty warm outside.

It was Christmas in Queensland and the beer tasted like Australia. Strong and dry and producing a sigh of momentary content. He noted some corny Christmas music on the CD player and Maeve was holding one hand over her left ear, pleading for it to stop. Tara was laughing and Louisa looked offended.

He leaned towards her. 'So you don't like carols?'

'Not twenty-four seven for the last month,' she whispered. 'Save me.'

He laughed. And gave her a quick squeeze as she went past with another jug of sauce to put on the end of the table. She glanced back and she looked at him like he'd given her a present. *Be careful there,* he thought to himself. Expectations and what he could actually deliver could differ.

Angus came up and stood beside him. Raised his glass. 'Lemonade. I'm on call.' He grimaced. 'But cheers. I hear you're staying.'

'Cheers.' He lifted his beer. 'Staying until after the baby at least.'

'Good.'

That was unexpected approval. 'Thank you.'

'It's for Maeve. And Simon. But I'm guessing it's not all easy on your side either. Not easy to get used to all this when you didn't expect it.'

Rayne glanced around. 'It's taking some.'

Angus nodded. 'Just chill. This place is good

at helping the chill factor. Maeve has a lot of support so you won't be doing it on your own. And Tara is a good midwife.'

Change of subject. Great. 'Which reminds me. Congratulations on your new daughter-in-law-to-be. I haven't seen Simon look this happy, ever.'

Angus nodded. Glanced at his son, who had Tara's hand clasped firmly in his. Tara was laughing up at him. 'Best Christmas present I could wish for.' Then he glanced at his own wife and daughters. 'Finding the right woman is hard but incredibly worth it.'

'Okay, everyone,' the woman he was regarding said. 'Sit.' He inclined his head at her, gave Rayne a faint smile, and moved away to hold Louisa's chair, and then his wife's. He sat at the head of the table and Louisa sat on his left, with Mia on his right.

Simon sat at the other end with Tara next to him and Maeve on the other side. Rayne was in the middle opposite the two little girls, who were giggling at something Simon had said.

After this morning, he wasn't surprised when the elder of the two girls said grace, and for a fleeting moment he wondered with an inner smile whether, if he had a daughter, he would ever hear her piping little voice bless this table at Christmas. His throat thickened and he drew a quiet breath, and in a reflex he couldn't control he blocked it all out. Blocked out the tinny Christmas music, the laughing people, the beautiful woman expecting his baby beside him.

Maeve felt the distance grow between her and Rayne and wanted to cry. There had been moments there when he'd seemed to be settling into the day better than she'd expected. Especially when she'd noted his obvious rapport with Louisa, but, then, who didn't feel that? Louisa was a saint. Even when she'd first arrived and been at her most prickly and morose, Louisa's gentle, good-natured kindness had won her round before she'd known it.

She'd seen him talking to Angus. Well, since she'd arrived she'd decided Angus was a man's man, so that wasn't surprising. Rayne hadn't really spoken to the girls or Mia since they'd been introduced, but in fairness he hadn't had much chance. She couldn't help hoping he would exhibit some signs he was good with children. The guy was a paediatrician, for goodness' sake. And soon to be a father.

Tara leaned across the table and distracted her by offering the end of a Christmas cracker to pull. 'I'm not sure how many of these I'm supposed to pull,' she said in a quiet aside. 'I just did it with Simon and of course he won. And with Amber and she won. But I want a hat.'

Maeve smiled. 'You can pull any bon-bon offered. It's the bon-bon owner's choice who they want to pull them with. So take any you can.' Maeve had pulled a lot of bonbons in her time.

The two young women had tested their strength against each other, and Tara had been a little more competitive than Maeve had expected, and that made her smile.

Maeve pulled harder and the bon-bon banged and split in half. Tara got the bigger half and the hat and prize. This time Tara crowed as she won. Simon clapped. He didn't miss much where Tara was concerned, Maeve thought with a pang. She glanced at Rayne. He was watching but his face was impassive and she got the feeling he wasn't really there.

Not so flattering when she was sitting beside him. 'Would you like to pull a bonbon with me?' Darn, did she have to sound so needy?

He blinked. 'Sorry?'

'A Christmas cracker.' She waved the one that was on her plate. 'See who wins.'

'Oh. Right. Sure.'

Such enthusiasm, she thought, and realised

she was becoming a crotchety old woman by waiting for Rayne to behave like her fantasies.

'It's okay. Don't worry. I'll pull it with Tara. She loves them.' She meant it. No problem. Then he surprised her.

'Oi. I love them, too.'

That was the last thing Maeve had expected him to say. 'You love bon-bons?'

'Yeah. Why not?' His eyes crinkled and she sighed with relief that he was back with her. 'Not like I had that many family lunches over the years. That Christmas at your place was the first. You made me coconut ice.'

He remembered. The thought expanded in ridiculous warmth. 'I made everyone coconut ice at Christmas. For years. But it's very cool that you remembered.'

He held his hand out for the end of her Christmas cracker and she waved it around at him. 'I want to win.'

They pulled it and Rayne won. 'Oops,' he

said. 'Try mine.' They realigned themselves to pull again and she could tell he tried hard to let her win but the cracker broke the larger end on his side. He got the prizes. Life sucked when you couldn't even win in a cracker-pull.

'Can I give it to you?'

'Not the same.' Shook her head. Pretended to be miffed.

He raised his brows. 'But I can't wear two hats.'

Then she said, 'Men just don't understand women.'

Rayne looked at the woman beside him, 'I'm hearing you.' He held out the folded hat. She took it reluctantly, opened it out and put it on. He'd given her the red one to match her dress and she looked amazing in a stupid little paper hat. How did she do that? He felt like an idiot in his.

He decided to eat. It seemed they were last to

reach for the food again but, then, they'd made inroads into the basket Louisa had sent with them to the lake. He was starting to feel sleepy and he wasn't sure if it was the fact he'd driven all night, though he'd slept most of yesterday after the flight. Or maybe Louisa's rum balls were catching up with him. He stifled a yawn.

'I'm a bitch.'

The piece of roast turkey that was on the way to his mouth halted in mid-air. 'Sorry?'

'You're tired. I'd forgotten you haven't slept.'

He had to smile at her mood swings. The idea that life would not be boring around Maeve returned with full force.

They ate companionably for a while, he answered a question from Louisa on how the drive had been and gradually relaxed a little more with the company. 'I'll snooze later. Isn't that what everyone does after Christmas lunch? Wash up and then lie around groaning and doze off until teatime?'

'You're eating off a paper plate. The washing up's been done.' She smiled at him and his belly kicked because he was damned if there wasn't a hint of promise in that smile. More than a hint.

She bent her head and spoke softly into his ear. 'Not everyone sleeps.'

Geez. He wasn't making love with Maeve when Simon's room was two doors down. Imagine if she went into labour and everybody knew he'd been the one responsible for the induction. His neck felt hot and he couldn't look at anyone at the table.

'Rayne?' She laid her hand on his leg and it was all he could do not to flinch. Since when had he ever been at this much of a loss? The problem was his libido was jumping up and down like a charged icon on a computer.

She yawned ostentatiously and stood up. 'Happy Christmas, everyone. I think I'll go put my feet up.'

'Bye, Maeve.' From Simon and the girls.

'Don't go into labour, Maeve. I'm too full,' Tara said.

She turned back to Rayne. 'You coming? I think we need to talk some more.'

His ears felt hot. He needed to get himself back on an even footing here. It seemed she'd turned into a militant dominatrix and while the idea of submitting to sex wasn't too abhorrent, it didn't fit with the very late pregnancy visual effect. And he wasn't enamoured by the smothered smiles of his lunch companions.

'Sure. I'll just help Louisa clear the table first.'

She narrowed her eyes at him. 'Fine.'

Hell. She'd said, *'Fine.'* Which meant she was emotional and he might just have heard a tiny wobble in the word, which meant maybe he should go and comfort her.

Louisa shooed him away. 'You cleared at breakfast. Off you go and help that girl put her feet up.'

He caught Simon's perplexed glance at his

grandmother and then at him. They both shrugged. How did you help someone put their feet up? Either way, he'd had his marching orders from two women. Maybe he should get his own place or they'd have him emasculated before New Year.

He stood up. Gave Simon a mocking smile and walked after Maeve.

CHAPTER SEVEN

Resting after lunch

MAEVE HAD GOT as far as slipping her shoes off, she'd been stupid, telling him to follow her, and she'd better learn from her mistakes pretty damn quick if she didn't want to drive him away.

She stewed on that thought for a minute until she heard Rayne's quiet footsteps coming down the hall and she didn't know whether to sit on the bed, stand at the window, looking decorative, or just freeze where she was looking at the closed door like a rabbit in headlights.

Time took care of that because Rayne knocked, paused and then opened the door and put his head around. She didn't get time to do anything except feel her heart thumping like a bass drum.

It was the Rayne from nine months ago. Black brows slightly raised, eyes dark and dangerous, a tiny amused tilt to those wicked lips. 'Louisa said you needed a hand to get your feet up?'

She licked dry lips. 'You can come in.' But when he did push open the door and shut it again the room shrank to the size of a shoebox and they were two very close-together shoes. 'Um. I am a bit tired.'

He glanced at the queen-sized bed then back at her. Looked her over thoroughly. 'Want a hand getting your dress off?'

'Thanks.' She turned her back and once he'd worked out there was no zip and she only wanted him to help her lift it over her head, the task was accomplished in no time.

No real seduction in that swift removal. She tried not to sigh. While he was draping the dress carefully over the chair she was thinking as she sat on the bed, *Thank goodness I changed my stretchy granny undies for the cute lace pair.*

He seemed to be staring at her chest. 'Nice cleavage.' Well, at least he appreciated something.

He was so big and broad standing over her and she patted the quilt she was sitting on. She wished he'd take off *his* shirt. 'Are you staying?'

'Staying? As in coming to bed with you?'

'You did say everyone lies down after Christmas lunch?'

He sat on the bed beside her. Then he turned his head and looked her full in the face. 'I'm not going to have sex with you but I'm happy to lie beside you while you rest.'

She pulled a face at him. Her own desire to snuggle up to him was withering like a dehydrating leaf. 'I wouldn't want to force you to do anything you didn't want to.'

He grinned at her but there was a definite flare in his dark eyes that left her in no doubt she was wrong. A flare that made all the saggy disappointment feelings sit up and take notice again. 'It's not that I don't want to get closer.' He was telling the truth and at least that made her feel a little bit better. 'But I think we need to talk a whole lot more before we fall into...' he hesitated, didn't even offer a word for what they were both thinking about '...first.'

Talk? When she was sitting here in her lacy bra and panties—admittedly with a huge shiny belly out in front—behind a closed door with all those pregnancy hormones saying ooh-ah. 'Talk?' She fought back another sigh. 'That sounds more like a girl thing than a guy thing.'

He shrugged, stood up again and then leaned down, slipped an arm behind her knees and the other under her shoulders and placed her in the middle of the bed. Oh, my, she loved the way he did that.

Then he bent, unlaced his shoes and removed them, loosened his belt and then sat back down on the bed in his jeans. Reached for the folded light sheet at the bottom of the bed she'd been resting under in the afternoons, swung his legs up and draped the sheet over both of them.

Then he slipped his arm around her shoulders so her head was resting on his chest and settled back.

She was still smarting from the 'not having sex with you' comment. 'Is this the pillow talk I missed out on last time?'

He didn't seem perturbed. 'You do have a nasty little bite when you don't get your own way, don't you?'

She hunched her shoulders. 'It comes with not knowing where I stand.'

'Well,' he said slowly, 'I see that. But I can't tell you what I don't know. And if you want me to make something up then you're resting your head on the wrong chest.'

It was not what she wanted to hear and yet it was. And this particular chest felt so good to lean on. She relaxed and snuggled in a little closer. 'So you're saying you won't lie to me.'

The sound of his heart beating in a slow, steady rhythm reverberated under her ear. God, she'd missed this. 'I won't lie to you.'

She lifted her other hand slowly and ran her fingertip down the strong bulge of his bicep. An unfairly sexy bicep. Her girl parts squirmed in remembered ecstasy. Conversation. Remember conversation. 'Not lying to me is a good start.'

'You're supposed to say you won't lie to me either.' She could tell he was dead serious. Fair enough.

She wriggled awkwardly, trying to shift her weight until she'd managed to roll and could see his whole face. Said just as seriously, 'I will not lie to you.'

She couldn't read the expression in his eyes but his mouth was firm. 'So if you want me to go, you tell me. Not telling me is a lie too.'

She frowned at him. 'I'm not sure I want to

hear about it if you want to go.' Then she sighed and lay back down again. 'But I guess that's fair.'

He was shaking his head. 'You don't understand and you need to get where I'm coming from. I may not be good at this whole father thing, Maeve. I'll try but I don't have a lot of family experience, and no paternal role model, to draw on.' She could hear the slight thread of panic in his voice. Had to remind herself that a few hours ago this guy had had no idea he would be having a child some time in the next few days.

She thought about his 'no family experience' statement. Well, she guessed he'd never had a father to learn from or even subconsciously copy. Maybe he was finding that pretty daunting. 'Did you know your father at all?'

'Nope. I asked. All my mother said was he was dead and didn't offer any clues. Not even his name. And my mum wasn't into men staying over so no "special" uncles. If she spent the night with a man, she usually stayed out.'

Maeve thought about that. 'So when you were young you stayed home alone? At night?'

Maeve squeezed his arm in sympathy and Rayne could feel himself begin to freeze her out. Had to force himself to let her offer comfort because if he was going to try to make this work he had to at least attempt to learn to do these things too. Apparently it was what families did and he needed to at least give it a shot.

He dispelled the myth that he had been alone. 'We lived in a dingy block of flats. You were never alone. You could always hear people in the other units.'

She nodded against him. 'So you never got scared on your own at night?'

He nearly said no. But he'd said he wouldn't lie. 'When I was younger I got scared. Especially if someone was shouting or I could hear someone yelling on the footpath. The worst was if a woman screamed down on the street. I always worried it was my mum and I wasn't doing anything to help her.'

He'd never told anyone that. Didn't know why he'd told Maeve. He moved on and hoped she would forget he'd said it. 'Guess I'd make sure my kid was never left alone until they wanted to be left.'

She squeezed him again. 'Perhaps your mum thought the people she was with were more disturbing than the idea of you being alone.'

His mum had actually said something like that. He hadn't believed her. Had there been a grain of truth in it after all? And Maeve had picked up on it all these years later. 'You don't judge her, do you? My mother?'

Maeve shrugged on his chest. 'Who am I to judge? I know nothing about her. I just know I've always admired you and she must have had a part in that. She was your mother.'

That heavy carpenter's rasp was back down

his throat. Sawing up and down and ripping the skin off his tonsils. Or at least that's what it felt like as his throat closed. He searched for some moisture in his mouth. 'Even when I said I'd been in prison because of her, you were sad for me that she was dead.'

He'd been thinking about that a lot. Couldn't get his head around the fact that Maeve saw the part of him he hadn't shown to many people. Except Simon. But he doubted her brother would have discussed it with his little sister.

She snuggled harder and his arm protested and began to cramp. He told it to shut up.

Then she said, 'Even though you didn't meet your father, I think you'll be a good dad. And you certainly tried to look after your mum from a very young age. You're probably better father material than many men who had dads.'

He grimaced at the fact that maybe he had become a little parental with his mum, but that didn't change the fact he hadn't been able to save her.

Maeve was like a dog with a bone. 'You'll be fine. You're a paediatrician so at least you're good with kids.' She settled back. The law according to Maeve.

'At least I'm that,' he said dryly. 'I'm good with sick kids.' And especially the ones who were left alone and needed company.

She went on, 'I was too young to understand about how you grew up. You always looked tough and capable when I saw you.'

Rayne listened to her voice, the husky tigress lilt tamed a little now, and thought about what she'd said. So he'd appeared tough and capable. He guessed he had been. By the time she'd been in her early teens he'd almost grown out of his, and his mum had begun to need a bit more care taken of her. A couple of dangerous overdoses. A problem with her supplier that had left her badly bruised. The way she'd forgotten to eat. She'd had two close shaves with the law and had told him if she ever got convicted she would die if she went to prison.

The last years had been a downward spiral and he'd tried most things to halt it. The number of rehab centres, fresh towns, health kicks they'd tried. Things would go well for a few months and he'd get tied up at work. Miss a couple of days dropping in then she'd start to use again.

The best she'd been had been in Santa Monica. She'd looked young for the first time in years. Had got a job as a doctor's receptionist at one of the clinics he worked from in the poorer area, a place where kids who needed care they normally couldn't afford could access a range of different doctors. And she'd been good at it.

She had connected well with the people who didn't need anyone to look down on them. He'd valued the once a week he'd donated his time there, away from the upmarket private hospital he'd worked in the rest of the time. And he'd cheered to see her making a life for herself. Fool.

Until the day she'd worked and gone home early. It had been his day as well and he'd finished late. Locked up. The investigation had been well in progress by the time he'd found out all the drugs had been stolen. Had known immediately who it had been. He hadn't been able to track her down anywhere until finally she'd rung him. Pleading. Promising she would never, ever, touch anything ever again, if he would say it was him. That this was her chance to go clean for life.

He'd hoped maybe it was true and that she would stop using. Then had begun to realise the fingers had been pointing to him anyway. So he'd made a conscious decision to try a last attempt at saving her.

He'd tried ringing Simon so he wouldn't find out from someone else that he would probably be going to prison. Hadn't been able to give the explanation on the phone and had had that ridiculous idea to fly out, explain and then fly back in twenty-four hours. He'd thought he should have just about that much time before it all came crashing down. Before the police came for him!

'Hey,' Maeve whispered, but she wasn't talking to him. The belly beside him rolled and shifted and his eyes fixed on the movement, mesmerised. He glanced quickly at Maeve, who was watching him with a gentle smile on her face, lifted his hand and put his palm on the satin skin. And the creature below poked him with something bony.

Geez. He looked back at Maeve.

'Cool, isn't it?' she said softly. And put her hand over his. And he realised with a big shift of emotion that the three of them were together for the first time. 'He likes you.'

His eyes jerked to her face. 'It's a he?'

She laughed. 'I really don't know. Just find

myself calling him he. Maybe because you weren't here.' He winced at that.

'Might be a girl.' She shrugged. 'I really don't care which.'

'I hope she looks like you.'

She looked at him as if she were peering over a pair of glasses at him. 'Why on earth would you want your son to look like me?'

'Okay. A boy could be like me but it would be very sweet to have a little girl who looks like you.' Then he spoilt it all by unexpectedly yawning.

She laughed. 'You need a nap more than I do. Why don't you take your jeans off? We can talk more later. Then you can roll over and I'll cuddle you.'

'Bossy little thing.' But suddenly he felt morbidly tired and he did what he was told, not least because his arm had gone totally to sleep now and his jeans were digging into him.

When he climbed back onto the bed and rolled

to face the door, she snuggled up to him as close as her big tummy would allow. It actually felt amazing when his child wriggled against him. Geez.

Maeve listened to Rayne's breathing change and she lay there, staring at his dark T-shirt plastered against his strong shoulders as he went to sleep.

She tried to imagine Rayne as a little boy, from a time when his first memories had begun to stick. Dark, silky hair, strong little legs and arms, big, dark eyes wondering when Mummy would be home.

It hurt her heart. She wanted to hug that little boy and tell him she'd never leave him scared again. How old had he been when his mother had begun to leave him? She had a vague recollection of hearing Simon say to her parents that Rayne's mum hadn't started using drugs until after something bad had happened when Rayne had gone to school.

She wondered what had happened to Rayne's poor mum. Something that bad? It couldn't have been easy, bringing up a child alone with very little money.

Her childhood had been so blessed. Always her hero brother Simon and three older sisters to look after her, as well as both well-adjusted parents, although her mum was pretty definite on social niceties.

Her dad was a fair bit older than her mum, but he'd always been quietly there, and her mother had come from a wealthy family and always been a determined woman. She'd been spoilt by her dad, but had sometimes felt as if she wasn't quite enough of a star for her mother. Hence the try-hard attitude she really needed to lose.

She would be thankful for all her blessings of family and now having this gorgeous, damaged man appear just when she needed him. He hadn't run. He'd promised to stay at least until after the birth. Had tried to fit into a strange family's Christmas Day, which must be pretty damn hard when he was still reeling from being in prison and adjusting to society again, and he'd just found out he'd fathered a child.

She stared again at the powerful neck and short hair in front of her eyes and the way the thick strands clung to his skull like heavy silk. Resisted the urge to move her hand from around his chest to touch it as she didn't want to wake him, but her fingers curled.

She could imagine her baby having hair just that colour, though, of course, hers was black like her dad's as well, so the kid didn't have much choice. But she would think of it as his father's hair. Would he have Rayne's eyes and mouth too?

Imagine.

A long slow pulling sensation surged in her belly from under her breasts down to her pubic bone, growing tighter and then after a while easing off. Just one.

Braxton-Hicks. Practice contractions. Not painful. Just weird, as if the baby was stretching out straight. But she knew it wasn't. Soon they would come more frequently. Maybe for a couple of hours at a time and then stop. For a few days probably. She'd told other women this so many times, but it was strange when it was yourself you were reassuring.

This time she'd welcomed it without the accompanying flare of nervousness she'd been fighting for weeks. Giving birth was a job that needed to be done and now that Rayne was here the time was right. Whatever happened, whatever her birth journey was meant to be, Rayne would be there to share it all. The best Christmas present of all.

Rayne woke an hour later, straight from dreaming about Maeve. Like he'd woken nearly every day for the last nine months. Except this time he really had her in his arms, his hands really were cupping her glorious breasts, her taut backside really was snuggled into his erection, which was growing exponentially with confirmation of the contact.

They must have rolled in their sleep.

She murmured drowsily, not yet awake, and languidly backed into him a little more. Unconsciously, his hands slid over her belly, pulling her closer.

The little person inside that belly nudged him and he recoiled in startled appreciation of where his actions were leading. 'Sorry,' he murmured, and slid his hands down to the sides of Maeve's abdomen, but Maeve was having none of it. Took his hands and placed them back on her breasts. Wriggled into him.

'Have mercy, Maeve,' he whispered in her ear, but he couldn't help the smile that grew on his face. She wriggled against him again and he groaned. Slid his rear end across the bed to make room for her to shift and turned her to face him. 'You are a menace.'

'And you feel so good against me,' she whispered back drowsily. Then tilted her face for a kiss, and there was no way he could resist those lips, that mouth, or keep it to one kiss. And the gentle salute turned into a banquet of sliding salutations and memories that resurfaced from all those months ago. How they matched each other for movements, timing, a connection between them that had him pulling her closer, but the big belly in the middle made everything awkward, yet erotic, and he must be the most debauched man on earth to want to make love to this woman who was so close to giving birth.

As if she'd read his mind, she said, 'If we don't make love now, you'll have to wait for ages.'

He really hadn't thought of that. 'Maybe we should wait.' But he seriously didn't want to.

And she obviously didn't. Nine months of fantasy and the woman of his dreams was demanding he make love to her.

No-brainer really.

In the Maeve fog that was clouding his mind he wasn't really sure what he'd been thinking to knock her back before.

Still in the fog, he slid from the bed, ripped his T-shirt off his head in one movement and kicked off his briefs. Knelt back down and dropped a big kiss right between Maeve's awesome assets. Geez, he loved her breasts.

He slid his hands around her back and unclasped her bra. Sighed as the two gorgeous spheres eased out of the restraining material like big, soft plump peaches. The circular areolas surrounding her nipples were dark peach, highlighted for a tiny baby to find easily, and he skimmed his fingers across in awe while she watched him with a womanly smile as old as the ages.

He swallowed to ease the dryness in his throat. 'They say pregnant women in the third trimester of pregnancy have erotic dreams and surges of erotic desires.'

'That's very true,' she whispered, pulling him closer and tilting her mouth for him to kiss again. When they paused for breath there was no concept of stopping. But he was doing this right, and gently, and he wanted to show her just how beautiful she was in his mind and in his heart. 'Then we'd better take our time.'

CHAPTER EIGHT

Labour and birth

WHEN MAEVE WOKE up Rayne was gone. But the contraction tightenings weren't gone. That darned love hormone.

She did not want to have this baby on Christmas Day. It was okay for baby Jesus. He'd never been materialistic, but Maeve knew how she'd feel about the one day of the year that belonged to everyone, in her corner of her world anyway. But it was her own fault.

Still, she could not regret this afternoon in Rayne's arms. She smiled a long, slow, satisfied smile. Regret definitely wasn't the word that sprang to mind.

Revel, ravish, rolling around with… Scraping

the bottom of the barrel there, but *reaaaalllyyy* amazing just about covered it. Her skin flushed at the thought of how wonderful he'd been, so unhurried, showing her a world of gentleness that had brought tears to her eyes. He had paid homage to her body, coveted her belly, and just plain loved her, something she'd missed so badly as her body had changed, and he had banished for ever the idea he wasn't the man for her.

Which was an excellent thing if she was about to have his baby.

Another contraction followed on the thought. That love hormone again.

She glanced at the clock. It was seven-thirty in the evening. Almost sunset. Less than five hours until midnight. 'Hang in there, baby.'

She climbed awkwardly out of bed. Pulled on a robe and gathered something light to wear for the evening. Something comfortable like a sarong. They'd probably sit out the back or go for a leisurely walk along the lake. Another contraction tightened her belly, this time with a little bit of discomfort.

They were still not lasting long but she guessed she wasn't going to go too far from home. At least there was no car journey involved, like there would have been if she lived in the city. Here, they'd just pick up Tara from the room down the hall—she grinned at that, same house—then walk across the road to the birth centre. It was all pretty streamlined, actually. Almost a home birth without the organising of equipment involved.

Rayne would be stressed. Simon would worry. But she would be calm. Could be calm now because she deputised other people to do the worrying and from this moment on she would have faith in her body, in a natural process she was designed to achieve. It was exciting really. And Tara would be there. She giggled. She hoped Tara had digested her lunch by now.

She thought about giggles. That's right. In early labour you apparently felt like giggling. The fact labour had finally arrived after all the waiting. Happy hormones. She grinned in the mirror. Actually, she did feel like giggling. Even the fact that she knew this would pass onto harder and stronger contractions was funny. At the moment, anyway. No doubt she'd change her mind later.

She slipped out of the bedroom door and into the bathroom with a smile on her face. She could hear the rumble of Simon and Rayne's voices coming from the kitchen. The thought made her feel warm. She would not have believed the change in her world in the last day. It was like she'd been released from her own prison. That thought put her feet back on the ground. She shouldn't joke about it. Rayne really had been released from prison.

She hung the robe on the hook at the back of the door, climbed into the shower and relaxed again as she revelled—there was that word again—in the hot water that soothed any tension away from her shoulders. Another contraction started its slow rise in intensity and consciously she sent all the negative thoughts down the drain with the soapy water, and breathed out.

Still ten minutes apart, plenty of time to tell people. She just wanted to hug the excitement and her baby to herself. This was the last day that she and her baby would be together so intimately. A miracle in itself.

She stayed in the shower for a long time.

Until Rayne knocked on the door. 'You okay in there?' A hint of concern in his voice.

She had to wait for the contraction to stop before she could answer. They were getting stronger but that was a good thing. More powerful, not more painful, she reminded herself. A tiny voice inside muttered about that not being true but she ignored it. The pain eased.

'I'm fine.' Wow. Her voice sounded kind of spacy. Endorphins.

'Can I come in?'

'Sure,' she breathed. Then had to repeat it a bit louder. 'Come in.'

Rayne pushed open the door and a cloud of steam billowed out past his head. He waved it away and stepped into the bathroom. 'You've been in here for ages.' He crossed the tiles to the corner shower. Stood outside the curtain. 'Is there something I should know?'

He waited. She didn't answer and he could hear her breathing. Eventually he pulled back the curtain so he could see her. She smiled at him and he thought she looked almost half-asleep. Looked again. Now, that was something you didn't see every day. A glistening wet, very rounded, amazingly breasted, porcelain pregnant lady naked in the shower, with her black hair curling on her shoulders.

She said, 'If we ever live together, you'll need a very large hot-water system.'

He had to smile at that. He assumed Louisa did own one of those if this house could sleep twelve. 'I'm getting that.'

'And also,' she went on in the same distant voice, 'my contractions are about seven minutes apart.'

His heart rate doubled and then he slumped against the wall. Sex fiend. He'd done that. Come on. Pull yourself together. You're a doctor, for crikey's sake.

'Is that a good thing?' he asked cautiously. Who knew what Maeve was thinking? He was trying to be supportive because that was his job, and he'd agreed without coercion when, in fact, he wanted to run screaming to Simon.

'As long as baby waits till after midnight, that's fine.'

Rayne glanced at his watch. Eight o'clock. Four hours until midnight. Of course she'd have her own way and the baby would wait. Four hours of stress.

'Shall I go and tell Simon? Or Tara?'

'No hurry.'

It was all very well to say that, along with some heavy breathing, and he observed, as if from a long way away, that his fingers were white where he was clutching the handrail. 'You sure?'

'Mmm-hmm...' Loud exhalation.

Geez. Rayne prised his fingers off the towel rail and straightened off the wall. 'Um. Might just mention it to them in case they want to go out.' Though where they would go on Christmas night was a mystery.

Quietly, on an out breath, an answer came from the shower. 'Okay.'

Rayne left and he wasn't quite jogging. He skidded into the kitchen but it was empty. Typical. This house had crawled with people all day and now he couldn't find anyone when he needed them. Even Louisa was missing but he guessed she, out of all of them, deserved a rest.

Poked his head out the back door but the darkening yard, a space that had seen so many Campbells, was deserted.

He went back inside, walked down the hallway, but both Simon and Tara's doors were ajar and he guessed if they were in there they'd have closed the doors. He went out to the front veranda in case they were sitting on that bench, looking at the nodding animals, and he was distracted for a minute by the fairy-lights that had come on with the sunset. Nobody there. He glared at the manger. Mary and Joseph had had their baby in a manger, with animals and wise men, so what was his problem?

He ran his hand distractedly through his hair. Took a deep breath. It was okay. Maeve was calm. Happy even. The hospital was across the road for pity's sake. He could see the porch lights. All he had to do was be a support person.

It would have been nice to have that 'couples' discussion with Tara that he'd had a knee-jerk reaction about today before Maeve had gone into labour. But, *no-o-o*, Maeve had had to have nookie.

What was it he'd learnt in med school? A first-time mum, after a slow start while the contractions got sorted out, dilated about a centimetre an hour. To get to ten centimetres was ten hours. Right? Or maybe she was already six centimetres then it would be four hours. Or less if she'd got there this quickly. His mind was spinning faster than the wheels of the new Christmas pushbike some happy, oblivious-to-the-drama-inside kid was pedalling past too late to be out.

He forced himself to take another breath. Yesterday he would not have believed all this was going to happen. Yesterday he had been wondering if she would see him. Today she was his responsibility.

Well, he'd been in at the beginning so he had to stay for the hard part.

'Rayne?' He spun round and Maeve was leaning on the door to the front veranda. She looked like she'd just stepped off a plane from Fiji, with a hibiscus sarong wrapped around her and not much else. He could see her cleavage from here.

'Why are you staring at the manger?'

He wasn't looking at the manger now. Cleavage. 'Umm. Looking for Tara and Simon.'

She leant her head on the doorframe. 'They're on the side veranda outside their rooms, watching the stars come out.'

He strode back across the lawn and up the steps to her side. 'Okay. You okay?'

'I'm fine. But I'd sort of like you to stay with me.'

'Yep. Of course.' He was obviously really bad at this support-person caper. Where was the midwife? 'So did you tell Tara?'

'I wanted to find you first.'

Not the choice he would have made. 'Fine. Let's do it now.'

'You said *fine*...'

She leant against his arm and smiled up at him and as if she'd pressed a button he leant down and kissed her lips in an automatic response. Just one day and they had an automatic response?

He stepped back. Must have picked up on some of her endorphins because he could feel his panic settle a little. *Fine.* Yep, he had been feeling freaked out, insecure, neurotic and emotional.

His voice softened, lowered, and he gently turned her back towards the house. 'How can you be so calm?'

'I've had nine months to think about this happening. You've had twelve hours.'

Had it only been twelve hours? It felt like twelve days. But, then, that's how things seemed to happen around Maeve and him. Acceleration with the pedal pressed and they were driving off into the future at a hundred miles an hour.

'Do you do anything slowly?' he said as they walked down the hall. He grinned at her. 'Apart from the way you're walking up the hallway now.'

'I put my make-up on slowly.'

'Does that mean if I took you out I'd be one of those guys hanging around waiting for his woman to get ready?'

'I might speed up for you.' Then her face changed and she stopped, closed her eyes as she leant against him. He lifted his hand and rested it on her arm and her shoulder dropped its tension beneath his fingers as if he'd told her to relax, and it startled him.

She sighed out, 'Boy, I can tell these contractions are doing the job.'

That was good. Wasn't it? 'We still waiting for midnight?'

'No choice now. It's all up to baby. You just have to hold my hand for the ride.'

He could do that. Glanced down at her hand, thin and suddenly fragile looking, as they set off again. 'It would be an honour,' he said very quietly. And it would be. She was blowing him away with her strength and serenity.

Simon and Tara, also holding hands again—spare me, he thought—appeared in the hallway and Maeve had a contraction before he could say anything.

Tara let go of Simon's fingers with a smile and went towards them. No need to say anything. So he didn't. Wasn't really his place anyway.

And they didn't ask. Their restraint was amazing and he could only follow their lead.

When the contraction was over, Tara murmured, 'Good job. When did they start?'

'About an hour ago.'

'So what do you feel like doing?' Tara was

walking beside Maeve as they drifted down the hallway to the kitchen. Simon smiled at Rayne.

'You should see your face.'

'Shut up.' But there was relief and he felt the smile cross his own face. 'Geez, mate. Yesterday none of this was happening.'

'I know. In that context you're actually doing well. But open your letters next time.'

Rayne gave him a hard look. 'Try being where I was and you might not feel so sure about that.'

The smile fell from Simon's face. 'You're right. But I would never do something as stupidly noble as that. But I should have known you would. I'm sorry I was so quick to believe in your guilt.'

Rayne heard Maeve laugh at something Tara had said and looked at Simon and dropped the whole subject. This wasn't about him. Or Simon. 'How can she laugh?'

They both walked towards the kitchen. 'See, that's why I chose obstetrics over paediatrics.'

Rayne thought about the stress he'd been under already. 'You think giving birth is funny? It's a wonder you haven't been killed.'

Simon laughed again and it felt good to loosen the tension between them. The dynamics were certainly tricky. Especially if he didn't make the grade to stay around for the long haul. But he would worry about that later.

'Rayne?' Maeve's voice.

He quickened his pace and left Simon behind. 'I'm here.'

'I want to go in the bath and Tara thinks it might be easier if I don't have to move from this bath here to the one in the birth centre. So maybe we should go over there fairly soon.'

'Sounds sensible to me.' Sounded amazingly sensible. A hospital, or a birth centre at least with a hospital next door.

Louisa appeared. Caught on very quickly what was happening. 'I'll pack a hamper.'

He looked at her. Felt more tension ease from his shoulders. 'You have a feeding fetish.'

'Must have.' She winked at him. 'I'm too old for any other kind of fetish.'

Simon and the two girls looked at her in comical surprise but Louisa was off to do her stuff.

'I'll see you over there,' Tara said. 'I'll go ahead and run the bath and then come back. We can check baby out when you get there. Take your time, unless you feel you have to hurry.'

What sort of advice was that? Rayne thought with a little flutter of his nervousness coming back. He for one felt like they had to hurry. But Maeve was nodding and doing a go-slow. She didn't even look like making a move.

Simon said he'd leave them to it. Maybe go and see his dad and let him know what was going on.

Rayne watched him go and thought, So the obstetrician leaves? He looked towards Maeve's bedroom. 'Do you have a bag packed?'

'Yep.' She was just standing there with a strange little smile on her face, looking out the window at the Christmas fairy-lights in the back yard. The clock on the wall ticked over a minute. And then another. He felt like ants were crawling all over him.

'Um. You want me to go and get the bag?'

She turned her head and smiled vaguely at him. 'You could.'

So how was he supposed to find it? This must be the kind of stuff normal people talked about when they were planning to have a baby. People who had more than twelve hours' notice they were going to be a support person in a labour. The woman would say, "My bag is in my wardrobe if we need it. My slippers are under the bed." Bathroom kits and baby clothes would have all been discussed. Baby names!

He tamped down his panic again. 'Where is the bag?'

'Behind the door.'

At last. He could do something. He looked at Maeve as if she might explode if he left, and then turned and strode up the hallway for the bag. Was back within seconds.

'Do you need anything else?'

She blinked. Smiled. 'Are you trying to organise me?'

Sprung. 'Uh. Just making sure everything is ready when you want to go.'

'It's really important—' she was speaking slowly as if to a child who wasn't listening '—that the birthing woman is the one who decides when to go to the birth centre. She has to feel like she *needs* to be somewhere else before she leaves the place she feels safe in *now*.'

'So this is what you tell women in antenatal classes? About when they go to the hospital?'

'And the men,' she said with a patronising smile.

They went across to the birthing centre at nine o'clock. Walked across the road, slowly, because

Maeve had to stop every few minutes. The stars were out. Christmas night. The air was still warm and Maeve was wearing the sarong.

He had her overnight bag over his shoulder, the hamper from Louisa in one hand and Maeve's elbow in the other.

'It's a beautiful night,' Maeve said after a very long drawn-out breath.

Yes. Yes, beautiful, he thought. *Come on.* 'Yep. You okay?'

She had another contraction and they stopped again.

Tara met them at the door. Nobody else was in labour so they had the place to themselves.

The midwife on duty was over at the hospital but would come across for the birth.

Angus was the doctor on call for obstetrics and would wait outside the door in case they needed him. All these things he found out in the first three minutes because he had requests, too! He really didn't know if he could handle a lifetime of responsibility for Maeve. What if something went wrong?

Tara sent him to make tea because Maeve needed to go to the ladies and he was pacing outside the door.

He was back too quickly.

He could feel Tara's eyes on him and he looked at her.

'Maeve is low risk, Rayne,' Tara said. 'It's her first baby. She's here on the day before the baby is due. Her waters haven't broken. She has no infections. Her blood pressure is normal. She's only been in labour for two hours at the most.' A sympathetic look. 'Why are you worried?'

'It's my first baby too?'

'Sure. I get that.'

He didn't think she did. 'I'm a paediatrician. They only called me for the babies that might need help and I've seen a lot of very sick babies. I guess my idea of normal birth is a bit skewed.'

Or more than a bit, and in any case he'd only found out about this baby today.

'I get that too. But Maeve's baby will be fine.'

He wanted to believe that. 'What if it isn't?'

'Then we will manage. It's what we do.' She glanced around the homey birthing room for inspiration, or at least something that would reassure him. 'Why don't you check the equipment? And the resuscitation trolley? All the drugs on the trolley? Check the suckers and oxygen.'

He couldn't help his horror showing in his face. 'You haven't checked those?'

She actually laughed. 'Yes, Dr Walters, I have checked those. But I'm trying to distract you!'

'Oh.' Now he felt dumb. 'Sorry.' He put his finger under the collar of his T-shirt because suddenly it felt tight.

Tara's voice was gentle. 'Maybe doing those things would be helpful if Angus called you in an emergency in the next few weeks.'

He sighed. Get a grip. Thank goodness Tara did have a sense of humour. 'Sorry. It's just been pretty sudden. I'm not normally such a panic merchant.'

She looked at him. 'I have no doubt that's true. I think you've done exceptionally well, considering the scenario you've fallen into. But here's the thing.' Her voice dropped and her face was kind but serious and she glanced at the closed bathroom door. He started to wonder if Maeve and Tara had cooked up this pep talk for him between them.

He guessed he'd never know.

'I need you to be calm. I need you to be Maeve's rock. You don't need to say much— just be here. Agree with her. She really wanted you to be here. And hold her hand when she wants you to. Rub her back when she wants you to. Okay?'

He took a big calming breath. 'Okay.'

'No more panic vibes, please. And in the

meantime you can familiarise yourself with the equipment only if you need distraction.'

Okay. He got that. The bathroom door opened and Maeve came out. He sat quietly in the corner of the room while Tara felt Maeve's abdomen, discussed the lie of the baby, which was apparently pointing in exactly the direction and attitude they wanted, and listened to his baby's heartbeat.

Geez. That was his baby's heartbeat. Cloppety, cloppety, clop. It was fast. He knew foetal hearts were fast. But was that too fast?

Calm. He needed to be calm. Dissociate. That was the answer. Pretend it wasn't his baby. Okay. He felt calmer. In fact, he felt in total control. It was cool. Normal heart rate.

'Rayne?'

'Yes, Maeve.'

'Can you hear our baby's heartbeat?'

'Yes, I can. It seems very fast!'

Tara looked at him with eyebrows raised.

He racked his brains. 'Baby must be as excited as we are.'

Maeve laughed. 'That is so cute.'

Cute. Geez. He stood up. Might go check the equipment.

The next hour was traumatic.

Then Maeve decided to get out of the bath and the hour after that was even worse.

But baby was fine. Heart rate perfect, with no slowing after contractions. Rayne's heart rate slowed after the contractions because during the contraction it doubled. And not just because he was rubbing Maeve's back non-stop.

Between contractions Maeve was calm. Rational. Gathering her strength for the next wave. During contractions it was hell.

Noisy. Intense. Painful when she had his hand in hers and dug her nails in.

Tara was the rock. Quiet. Steady. Unflappable. Like the calm in the storm. He'd look across at her when a contraction was at its height and she would be smiling. Gentle and calm. This was Maeve's profession as well. How did these women do this day in, day out?

'I am so going to be at your birth, Tara,' Maeve ground out as the contraction finally eased.

'Good. We'll swap places.'

Rayne shook his head. How could they carry on a normal conversation when two minutes ago she was ready to rip all their heads off?

And then it was time to push. Eleven forty-five p.m. He looked at Maeve. It had been incredibly hard work. Perspiration beaded her brow, and he leant across and wiped it.

'Hey, Rayne,' she said softly. 'You okay?'

How could she possibly care about him when she was going through hell? 'As long as you're okay, I'm okay.'

'I'm fine.'

He smiled. 'I'm *fine* too.'

She smiled back wearily. 'Home straight now.'

There had been a bit of a lull in the contractions after a series of torrid strong ones. 'So why has it stopped?'

'Nature's way of giving us a break before the last stretch.' Then her face changed. 'Oh.'

The next twenty minutes would be forever etched in his mind. Angus was outside the door in case he was needed. He'd checked, but they didn't see him. Simon had arrived as well but was waiting to be invited in afterwards. He'd bet there was some pacing happening out there. As much as he was suffering in here, it would have been a hundred times worse imagining outside the door. Especially with the Maeve soundtrack they had playing.

With each pushing contraction a little more of the baby shifted down. The excitement was building and Maeve was much more focused now she could use the contractions to make things happen. If there was one thing his Maeve could do, it was make things happen.

Maeve was impatient. No surprise there. She moved position several times, kneeling, leaning on a ball, leaning on Rayne. Even sitting on the toilet, but that stressed him out until Tara smiled and put a towel over the toilet seat so he could stop envisaging his baby falling into the toilet bowl. But eventually they were standing beside the bed, and he could actually see the hair on his baby's head.

'You're doing well,' Tara said.

Well? Doing well? She was freaking amazing, incredible. 'Come on, Maeve. You're nearly there, babe.' He saw her glance at the clock and register it was a few minutes after midnight. She'd got what she wanted, and she looked at him.

Triumph, thankfulness and new determination, and he realised it would never be the same between them again. But that was okay.

He could admit she was stronger than him. In some ways, anyway. Maeve turned to face him. 'I want to sit back on the bed against the pillows.'

So he lifted her and put her back on the pillows. 'Love that,' she panted, and even in that moment their eyes met and she tempted him. Then she relaxed back against the pillows, hugging her knees, and gave one long outward sigh. And suddenly the crown appeared then a head of black hair, stretched into a face, one shoulder and then the other.

'Want to take it from here, Rayne?' Tara murmured, and he got it instantly. He stepped in and put his hands under his baby's armpits and, gently eased with the pressure Maeve was exerting, his baby entered the world with his own hands around him in a rush of belly, thighs, long legs and feet and a tangle of cord and water— and suddenly in a huge internal shift and crack through the wall of years of keeping emotion at bay, tears were streaming down his face.

Maeve was staring down with surprise and he lifted the squirming buddle of...? He glanced between the legs, grinned. 'It's a boy!' His eyes met hers and for that moment, when she looked at the baby, and then him and then the baby again, he didn't see how anything could ever stand between them.

His son cried. Loudly and lustily, and Maeve gathered him and snuggled him up against her breasts, and the baby's cries quieted instantly.

Boob man. Chip off the old block. He experienced such a swell of emotion his heart felt like it was going to burst.

In shock he saw the second midwife—where had she come from?—lean in to dry the little legs and arms and belly and rub the damp hair before she stepped back and replaced the damp towel with a warm bunny rug over them both until the baby was in a Maeve skin and bunny-rug sandwich.

Tara delivered the placenta and then a big warm hospital blanket covered Maeve's legs and belly and arms until finally her baby was tucked snugly with just his downy cheek against his mother, turned sideways toward Rayne, with big dark eyes and little squashed nose, and deep pink rosebud lips and a gorgeous mouth like Maeve's. And it was done.

His chest felt tight. 'Hello, there, buddy,' Rayne said softly.

He glanced at the clock. Ten past twelve. Boxing Day baby. Eighteen hours after arriving in Lyrebird Lake here he was—a father. New responsibility swamped him.

CHAPTER NINE

Emergency

MAEVE LAY THERE with the weight of her son on her chest, feeling the little wriggles on the outside of her body instead of the inside as he shifted. Could smell the unmistakable scent of new babies, and blood, and almost taste the relief in the room.

Why were they all worried? She had this. She looked at Rayne, who was sinking into the chair beside the bed that Tara had pulled up for him, unnaturally pale. His hand was halfway to the baby and hung suspended in the air as if he didn't know whether to touch or not.

'He's your son,' she whispered. Wishing he would kiss her. As if he'd heard her, he half stood and leaned across and kissed her lips. His hand drifted down and he touched the downy cheek of their child.

'Thank you. He's amazing. You were incredible.' He blinked a couple of times. 'Are you okay?'

'Buzzing,' she said, and grinned at him, and he shook his head and sank back in the chair. Looked like Rayne had aged ten years, she thought to herself. Still, the years sat well on him.

She glanced at Tara, who was taking her blood pressure. Waited until she was finished and then caught her hand. 'Thanks, Tara.'

Tara smiled mistily. 'I'm going to hold you to that promise.'

'Why? Because you know you'll be much quieter than me?'

Tara laughed. 'You always will be more outspoken than I am. You tell it like it is. Fabulous birth. I loved it.'

She glanced back at Rayne, who was looking at them both as if they were mad.

Tara said, 'Can Simon and Angus come in now? Then everyone will go away so you three can get to know each other.'

Maeve looked at Rayne, who left it up to her, so Simon and Angus came in.

After congratulations Tara took Angus aside, and Maeve could distantly hear that they were discussing the labour and birth, the blood loss, which had been a little more than usual but had settled now, and she saw Simon pump Rayne's hand.

'You look ten years younger, Simon.' Maeve teased him, as he leaned in to kiss her.

'I gave them to Rayne. You, sister, dear, are a worry that thankfully is not mine any more.' He slapped Rayne on the back. 'Welcome to parenthood, Rayne. It's never going to be the same again.'

Rayne still looked in shock. For a tough guy that was pretty funny. 'I get that premonition.'

'You look pale,' Simon said.

'I feel pale.' Rayne glanced across at the new baby, a baby with his own huge dark eyes and maybe it was his mouth.

Maeve remembered a new mother telling her once that when her baby had been first born she could see all the familial likenesses but after a couple of hours she'd only been able to see her baby as whole. Maeve tried to imprint the separate features before that happened. She could see his father's stamp as plainly as if there was a big arrow pointing to it. The brows and nose were from her side.

Rayne shook his head and smiled at her and she soaked up like a hungry sponge the amazed awe he was exuding in bucketloads. She must look a mess but for once she didn't care.

Maeve relaxed back in the bed, letting the euphoria wash over her. She'd always loved watching the way new mums seemed to have this sudden surge of energy, and now she was feeling it herself. She did feel that if she needed to, she could pick up her baby and run and save them both. Probably needed a few more clothes on for that, though, or she'd be scaring people.

She'd discarded the sarong hours ago. Clothes had seemed too much of an annoying distraction in the maelstrom of labour. Her baby wriggled and began to suck his fingers on her chest. His head lay between her breasts with his cheek over her heart, and she smiled mistily down at him. Next he would dribble on his fingers then he would start to poke and rub her with his wet hands as his instincts began to take over.

Yep, he was doing that now, she was careful not to distract him as his little head lifted and he glanced around.

Simon and Angus left and she barely noticed

as she saw her baby look and sniff for the dark areolas and the nipple he would find a way to arrive at.

'Watch him,' she whispered to Rayne, who leaned closer. 'He'll bob his head and wriggle and find his own way to where he needs to go.'

The baby's hands were kneading the softness of her breast under his tiny fingers, and his pink knees had drawn up under his belly as if he was going to crawl. 'Can't you just move him there?' Rayne said quietly.

'I could, but he needs to do a sequence. He needs to learn to poke out his tongue before he attaches, and he'll get there under his own steam at just the right moment.'

'He's only half an hour old.'

'That's why a baby stays skin to skin on his mother's chest for that first hour. Shouldn't get nursed by anyone else or have needles or get weighed or anything. It gives them the chance to do all this and the breastfeeding rates go through the roof if the baby attaches by himself. You watch.'

Baby was bobbing his head up and down like a little jack-in-the-box, and Maeve saw him narrow his gaze on the left nipple and lean towards it. Tiny jerking movements, and shoulder leans, and hand scrunching, and slowly his body changed angle, his neck stretched, and incredibly he was almost there. Another wriggle and head bob and stretch, a series of little tongue peeps as he began to edge closer.

'Come on, little guy,' his father whispered, and she had a sudden vision of Rayne on the sideline of a tiny tots soccer game, being the dad yelling, 'Go, son!'

'Do you like Connor as his name?'

Rayne looked at her. Grinned. 'Spelt with two ns.'

'Lord, yes. As much as I like the Irish version of Conor, this child will not go through life having to spell his name, like I did.'

'Or have people say "Rain, as in wet?"'

'I was teasing.'

'Beautifully.' He leaned across and kissed her and in that moment her world was complete. 'I think he looks very much like a Connor.'

'You can choose the second name.' She saw his face shutter. Felt the withdrawal.

'I didn't do enough to warrant that privilege.'

She felt the slap of reality right when she didn't want to. Acknowledged he was feeling inadequate, and maybe even vulnerable at the moment but, hey, she was the one with no clothes and had exposed herself to the world. She narrowed her eyes at him. 'Then try harder.'

She searched in her mind for a way to make him see that unless he wanted to, they would never lose him. 'Besides, he's going to cost you a fortune.'

He grinned and she saw the tension fall from his shoulders. Saw his look at her and the comprehension of how adroitly she'd manoeuvred him. Given him something he really could do, regardless of his parenting skills. His smile had a touch of the old bad-boy Rayne who'd been missing for the last few hours. 'In that case, how about the middle name of Sunshine?'

She knew he was kidding. She hoped he was kidding. 'Is that Sunshine from Rayne?'

Just then Connor found the nipple, poked out his tongue, opened his mouth wide and swooped. On! And didn't let go. Maeve gasped and smiled. 'That feels really weird.'

Rayne sat back in wonder. Tara leaned in from passing by and nodded. 'Good work, young man.'

'Connor.'

'Nice name. Welcome, Connor.' And she smiled at them both.

'Connor Sunshine.'

'Really?' She grinned at Maeve, who glared briefly at Rayne before looking back at her son. 'Awesome.' Then Tara had a brief feel of

Maeve's belly, to check her uterus was contracting, gave it a little rub, then went back to sorting the room and writing the notes.

'You should've seen your face.'

But Maeve had moved on. Was gazing down at her son, whose jaw was working peacefully, his hands each side of his mouth, fingers digging into her breast every now and then. And all the while his big dark eyes stared up into her face. A swell of love came out of nowhere. Like a rush of heat. Her baby. She would protect this tiny scrap of humanity with her last breath.

'He's incredible,' she whispered, and all joking disappeared as they both watched him.

The next fifteen minutes were very peaceful. They didn't talk much, mostly just stared, bemused at the new person who had entered their lives and would change them as people for ever.

Until Maeve felt the first wave of dizziness and realised the wetness beneath her was spreading and she was beginning to feel faint.

* * *

Rayne watched the downy jaw go up and down on Maeve's breast and marvelled at the dark eyes watching his mother. He could feel his heart thawing and it wasn't comfortable. Maeve had had his baby.

He thought about the last twenty-four hours. Driving to Lyrebird Lake, not knowing if she would see him. Or knowing if that powerful current between them from the night so long ago had been real or instigated by the events that he'd known would follow.

Then seeing her this morning, pregnant, catching her as she'd fallen, daring to calculate on the slightest chance it could possibly be his child when Maeve should never have conceived. His fierce exultation that had drowned out his shock.

The swell of emotion was almost a physical pain in his chest as he went over the last tumultuous few hours of labour and finally the birth. Now here he was. A father with his son. A helpless newborn with him as a father. At least Connor had a father.

'Take him, Rayne.'

'He's still drinking.' Rayne was glued to the spectacle but something in her voice arrested him.

'Started bleeding,' she said faintly. 'Get Tara.' Her eyes rolled back, and she fainted like she had when he'd first seen her, only this time he caught his son.

Rayne's heart rate doubled. 'Tara!' Hell. He scooped Connor off his mother's chest as Maeve's arms fell slack, wrapped him in the bunny rug that had covered them both under the big blanket and hugged him to his chest as he leaned over Maeve.

Connor bellowed his displeasure at being lifted off his mother and automatically he patted his bottom through the rug.

Tara scooted back to the bed from her little

writing table in the corner, lifted the sheet and sucked in a breath at the spreading stain on the sheets that just then flowed down the sides of the bed. 'Hit that red button over there for help and grab the IV trolley. We'll need to insert cannulas.' He saw her slide her hand over Maeve's soft belly, cup the top of her uterus through the abdominal wall and begin to rub strongly in a circular motion as he forced himself to turn away and do what needed to be done.

Once he'd pushed the emergency bell, he strode into the treatment room he'd cased earlier and grabbed the IV trolley and pushed it back towards the bed, not as fast as he'd have liked because it was awkward with his son tucked like a little football against his chest. Connor had stopped crying and when Rayne glanced down at him his dark eyes were wide and staring.

Put the cannulas in. That he could do. He glanced around for somewhere to put Connor.

Saw the little crib and tucked him in quickly. Connor started to cry.

'Sorry, mate.' He could find and secure veins on tiny infants so he should be able to do it on someone bigger. Someone he couldn't afford to lose.

'What size cannulas do you want?'

'Sixteen gauge. Two.'

Right. Found the size, the tourniquet, the anti-septic. Saw the tubes for blood tests. 'Which bloods?'

Another midwife hurried in after him and Tara glanced up and spoke to her. 'Get Angus back here first, then lower the bedhead so she's tipped down, give her oxygen, then draw me up a repeat ten units of syntocinon. Obs we'll get when we get a chance.'

Tara hadn't taken her hand off the uterus and the flow had slowed to a trickle but the loss from just those few minutes of a relaxed uterus had astounded Rayne with its ferocity. At least two litres had pooled in the bed.

She turned to him. 'Purple times two, one orange and one blue. Coags, full blood count, four units cross-match.'

'Angus is on his way,' the other midwife said, as she lowered the bed and slipped the oxygen mask onto Maeve's white face. 'Just some oxygen, Maeve.' The girl spoke loudly and as he withdrew the blood for the tests he realised Maeve might be able to hear.

'Hang in there, Maeve. Don't be scared. We'll get it sorted.' Incredibly his voice sounded confident and calm. Not how he was feeling on the inside. He wondered if Tara was as calm as she seemed.

Angus hurried in. Took over from Tara down the business end, checking swiftly to see if there was any damage they'd missed, but the sheer volume and speed of the loss indicated a uterus that wasn't clamping down on those powerful arteries that had sustained the pregnancy. Tara began assembling IV lines and drugs. She gave one bag of plain fluids to him and he connected and secured it. Rayne turned the flow rate to full-bore volume replacement until they could get blood.

An orderly arrived and the nursing supervisor who carried the emergency record started writing down times and drugs as she listened to Tara who spoke as she sorted the emergency kit.

The second midwife was writing Maeve's name on the blood-test tubes. When she was finished she wrote out a request form and sent the samples on their way. Then she hooked Maeve up to the monitor and they all glanced across at the rapid heartbeats shooting across the screen in frantic blips. Her blood pressure wasn't too bad yet but he knew birthing women could sustain that until it fell in a sudden plunge. His neck prickled in the first premonition of disaster.

Angus looked up at the second orderly. 'Bring back two units of O-neg blood. We'll give those until we can cross-match.'

'I'm O-neg if you need more.' Blood. She needed blood, Rayne thought, and wondered how often this happened for them all to be so smooth at the procedures. He glanced at Maeve's face as she moaned and began to stir with the increase in blood flowing to her brain from the head-down position change.

He wanted to go to her but Tara handed him the second flask loaded with the drugs to contract the uterus. 'Run it at two hundred and fifty mils an hour,' she murmured, and he nodded, connected it and set the rate. Then stood back out of the way. The whole scene was surreal. One moment he had been soaking in magic and the next terror had been gripping his throat as Maeve's life force had been seeping away.

'Given ergot yet?' Angus was calm.

'No. But it's coming.' Tara was drawing up

more drugs. Rayne's legs felt weak and he glanced across at Connor roaring in his cot. He picked him up and the little boy immediately settled. He hugged his son to him.

'You okay?' Angus looked at him.

No, he wasn't, but it wasn't about him. He crossed to sit back in the chair beside Maeve's head so he could talk to her as she stirred. They didn't need him staring like a fool and fainting, with his son in his arms. Couldn't imagine how frightening this would be for her. 'It's okay, sweetheart. Just rest. Angus is here.'

Her eyelids flickered and for a brief moment she looked at him before her eyelids fell again. 'Okay,' she breathed.

He looked at Angus. 'Why is she still bleeding?'

'Might be an extra lobe of placenta she grew that we missed.' Angus was massaging the uterus through Maeve's belly like Tara had been doing. 'Or could just be a lazy uterus. Or could be a tear somewhere. We'll try the drugs but if it doesn't settle, because of the amount of loss, we'll have to take her to Theatre.'

Angus glanced at the nursing supervisor. 'Call Ben and Andy, clue them in, and have operating staff standing by. We can always send them home.'

Nobody mentioned it was early Boxing Day morning. The supervisor nodded and picked up the phone. 'And phone Simon,' Angus said, with a quick glance at Rayne. 'We'll need his consent.'

Consent for what? Operating theatres? He could give that consent. No, he couldn't. He had no legal claim on Maeve or his son. He had nothing except Maeve's permission to be here. He was no one. Shook himself with contempt. It wasn't about him.

And what would they do? But he knew. They would do what they needed to do to save her life. And if Maeve could never have children again? He thought of the powerful woman who had majestically navigated the birth process with gusto. Imagined her distress if the chance would never be hers again.

He imagined Maeve dying and reared back from the thought. They would get through it. She had to get through it.

'She's started to bleed again,' Angus said to Tara. 'Get me the F2 alpha and I'll inject it into her uterus.' To the other midwife, he said, 'Check the catheter isn't blocked and I'll compress the uterus with my hands until we can get to the OR.'

The next two hours were the worst in Rayne's life. Worse than when they'd come for him in Simon's house and he'd seen Maeve's distress, worse than when he'd been sentenced to prison, worse than when he'd found out his mother had died.

Maeve went in and for a long time nobody

came out. Simon sat beside him in the homey little waiting room that was like no other waiting room he'd ever seen.

It had a big stone water cooler and real glasses to drink from. A kettle and little fridge to put real milk in your tea and a big jar of home-made oatmeal biscuits. And a comfortable lounge that he couldn't sit on.

He paced. Connor didn't seem to mind because he slept through it in his bunny rug. Rayne couldn't put him down. Not because Connor cried but because Rayne couldn't bear to have empty arms while he waited for Maeve to come through those doors.

'Do you want me to take Connor?'

'No!' He didn't even think about it. Looked down at his son asleep against his chest. Doing at least something that he knew Maeve would like while he waited. 'What's taking them so long?'

'She'll go to Recovery when they've sorted

everything. Then Dad will come through and talk to us. Or maybe Ben or Andy.'

'Are they good?'

'Superb.'

'I feel so useless. I worried about being a good enough father. That's nothing in the big picture.'

'It's not a nothing. But this is bigger. But you'll be fine. She'll be fine.'

Rayne heard the thread of doubt in Simon's voice and stopped. Looked at the man who would become his brother-in-law. Because he would marry Maeve. If she'd have him. He didn't deserve her. Would never have presumed to think she'd have him. But after this fear of losing her he'd take her faith in him and hold it and be the best dad a man could be. And the best husband.

Surely that would be the start of good enough?

He had a sudden vision of waking up in bed beside Maeve for every morning to come for the rest of his life. How the hell would he get out of bed?

But Simon. He'd forgotten that Maeve was the sister Simon was most protective about. How could he forget that in the circumstances? Because he needed to think of other people in his life now. He wasn't alone. He had Maeve, and Connor, and apparently a whole family or two. He glanced down at his son again and then at Simon.

He stopped where Simon was sitting. 'Can you hold him for a sec? My arm's gone to sleep.' It hadn't but he could see Simon needed something to hold as well. Tara was in the operating theatre with Maeve and she couldn't help him.

He watched his friend's face soften as he took the sleeping infant. Saw the tension loosen in the rigid shoulders. He missed the weight of Connor but was glad that Simon had him for the moment. Funny how a tiny helpless baby could help both of them to be stronger.

And then the doors opened and Angus came out. He looked at Simon first and then at Rayne.

'She had a spontaneous tear in her uterus. Probably a weakness in the muscle she was born with. It took a while to find it and she lost a lot of blood. But she's stable now.'

Rayne felt his body sag. Was actually glad that Simon held Connor.

'No more normal births for her. And a Caesarean in a bigger centre next time in case it does it again.'

So they had saved her uterus. Not bad for a tiny country hospital. 'So more blood transfusions?'

'And fresh frozen plasma and cryo. They'll need some of your blood over at the blood bank because we've used nearly all of theirs.'

It was the least he could do.

'Do we need to ship her out to a bigger hospital?' Simon had stood and his father was smiling at him with his nephew in his arms.

'I don't think so. And I would if I thought she needed to go. Would have spirited her there half an hour ago if I could have, but the crisis is past.' He grinned at Simon, who was swaying with the baby. 'Can't you men put that baby down?'

Rayne glanced at his friend. The relief was soaking in slowly. 'We're sharing the comfort. So she'll be fine?'

'She'll have to spend a few more days in hospital than she expected but she'll be spoiled rotten in Maternity.'

Rayne thought of going back to the manse without Maeve and Connor. 'Can I stay there, too? In the room with her and Connor? Help her with the baby?'

Angus raised his brows. 'Can't see any reason why not. Might mean that Tara will hand her over because she's not budging and I think she's nearly out on her feet.' He glanced at his son with a tired smile. 'Tara did a great job, Simon.'

So many amazing people here. So many he had to thank. Rayne stepped up to Angus and shook his hand. How could he ever repay them? 'Thank you. Thank the other guys.'

'We'll call in a favour if we need it.' Angus smiled.

Rayne looked at him. Saw a man who would be ruthless if he needed something for his little country hospital, and understood that. Smiled at it. Got the idea that resources could be hard to come by here when life threw a curve ball but those who had chosen to live here had saved his Maeve. They could have him any time they wanted.

He saw that he'd been accepted and was therefore fair game. He could deal with that. Thought for the first time about where Maeve might want to live and that, for the moment, if it was here he could cope with that.

Ten minutes later Simon took Tara home and Rayne carried Connor back to the room that would be Maeve's. The night midwife, Misty, took him through to the nursery and they finally got around to weighing Connor and giving him his needles, then she ran her hands all over him, checking that everything was fine.

She listened to his heart and handed the stethoscope to Rayne with a smile. 'Tara said you were a paed.'

Rayne listened. His son's heart sounded perfect. No valve murmurs. No clicks. He ran his own hands over him as if he were a baby he had been asked to check. But this wasn't a baby of some other lucky couple. This was his son. His hands stilled. This child depended on him for all the things his own father hadn't given him and he would deliver.

Misty handed him clothes and he looked at the tiny singlet. Thought of Maeve.

'Maeve's missing this. Wish she was here to share it.'

'Have you got your phone?'

He looked at her blankly. It wasn't like he could ring her. It must have shown on is face.

Misty laughed. 'You are tired. I can take photos of you dressing Connor and you can show her later.'

He shook his head. He should have thought of that. Handed her the phone in his pocket and Misty started snapping.

Rayne glanced at the sink as he lifted the singlet to stretch it widely over Connor's head. 'So when do we bath him?'

Misty shook her head. 'Not for twenty-four hours. He still smells like Mum and it helps him bond and feel secure and remember what to do when he goes for his next feed.'

Rayne vaguely remembered that from something Maeve had said, along with the skin to skin with Mum in the first hour.

Connor stared sleepily up at him as he dressed him. 'And what if he gets hungry before Maeve comes back?'

'He'll be fine. Tara said he fed well at birth. That's great. He could sleep up to twelve hours before he wakes up enough to feed again this first day. It's made such a difference letting them have that one long sleep after birth. Breastfed babies feed at least six to ten times a day and he'll catch up later.'

'I should know this stuff.' He shook his head. 'I've been out of it for nearly a year and in the States the doctors don't really discuss breast-feeding issues.'

She laughed. 'Everyone does everything here.'

He captured and pulled Connor's long fingers gently through the sleeve of the sleeping gown. All the experience came back as he turned the little boy over onto his front and tied the cords of his nightgown. Made him feel not so use-less. He could do this for Maeve. He folded the gown back carefully so it wouldn't get damp if he wet his nappy. 'Don't you use disposable nappies here?'

'Not until after they do their first wee. Those new disposables are too efficient and it's hard to tell sometimes.'

'Fair enough.' He clicked the pin with satisfaction and tugged the secure nappy. Good job.

Misty nodded approvingly. 'You can even do a cloth and pin nappy without help. Not many dads could do that the first day.' The phone rang and she handed him a clean bunny rug. 'Excuse me.'

She poked her head back into the nursery. 'They're bringing Maeve back now.'

Rayne felt relief sweep over him as he wrapped Connor and put him snugly back into his little wheeled cot. Tucked him under the sheets so he didn't feel abandoned. His eyes were shut. Misty had put nappies and wipes and assorted linen under there in case he needed it in the room overnight and Rayne trundled the cot out the door and down the hallway, where two men were pushing a wheeled bed into the room.

His first sight of Maeve made him draw in his breath. She looked like Snow White, icily beautiful, but deeply asleep and as white as the sheets she lay on with her eyes shut. Her black hair made her look even paler and his heart clutched in shock. Unconsciously his hand went down until he was resting it on Connor's soft hair, as if he needed the touch of his son to stay calm.

She stirred as the bed stopped against the wall of the room. Blinked slowly and then she opened her eyes, focused and saw him. Licked her dry lips. Then softly, barely perceptibly, she murmured, 'Hi, there, Rayne.'

'Hi, there, Princess Maeve.' He pulled the cot up to the side of the bed. 'Your son is beautiful.'

'Our son,' she whispered.

'I love him already.' He didn't know where the words had come from but he realised it was somewhere so deep and definite in him that it resonated with truth and the smile on Maeve's face as she closed her eyes assured him it was the thing she most wanted to hear.

'Then I can leave him to you while I sleep.'

'I'm here. I'm not going anywhere.'

'Thank you.' And she breathed more deeply as she drifted back to sleep.

He watched her chest slowly rise and fall. Glanced at the blood running into a vein in her left arm and mentally thanked the donor who had provided it. Checked the drugs running into a right-arm vein. Watched Misty as she straightened the IV lines, the monitor leads and the automatic blood-pressure machine, set to record every half an hour, until they were all in a position she could glance at every time she came into the room.

Rayne shifted his intended chair slightly so he could see too. Frowned over the fact that Maeve's heart rate was still elevated, her blood pressure still low. But respirations were normal. And even as she slept just a tinge of colour was returning to her face.

He pushed Connor's cot quietly towards the big chair beside the bed and sank back into it. Then pulled the cot halfway between the bed and the chair so that either of them could stretch out their arm and could touch their son. Then he settled down to watch Maeve.

CHAPTER TEN

MAEVE WOKE AND the room was quiet. It was still dark through the windows outside and her belly felt like it was on fire. At first she thought Rayne was asleep but he shifted and sat straighter when he saw she was awake and she wondered vaguely if he'd been awake all this time. Watching over her. It was an incredible thought.

'Hi.' She couldn't keep a frown off her face.

'Pain not good?'

She decided shaking her head would be too much movement. 'Eight out of ten.'

He stood up. 'I'll get Misty.' Left the room in a few long strides and she tried to lessen the tension in her body. What the heck happened to her beautiful natural birth? And how had she ended up being sore both ends? Now, that sucked. Closed her eyes and decided to worry about it tomorrow.

Misty came back in with Rayne and brought some tablets and a bottle of water with a straw.

Rayne slid his arm under her shoulders and eased her up so slowly and gently that it barely hurt to move. She swallowed the pills and savoured the water as it ran down her throat as he laid her down again.

Misty checked all her observations then Connor's, without rousing him, and then lifted the sheets and checked her wound and her bleeding and nodded with satisfaction at both. 'Looking beautiful.'

She heard Rayne, say, 'You midwives are weird.'

It would hurt to laugh. Misty laughed and left the room and Maeve smiled. She turned her head carefully and looked at Connor. Sleeping like a baby. Hugged that thought to herself then looked at Rayne, who was watching her. There was something different about him.

'You okay?'

He smiled and there was so much caring in the look he gave her that she felt herself become warm. 'I'm okay, as long as you are,' he said.

Meaning? 'Been a pretty torrid day?'

He stood up. Smiled down at her. Took her hand in his and turned it over. Careful of the IV lines, she thought. It was just a hand. Then he kissed her palm and it became a magic hand.

Then he said, 'A first for me as well. You scared the daylights out of me.'

Funnily, she hadn't been scared. 'I wasn't scared. You said not to be. Thank you for being there.'

He shook his head. 'Connor is amazing.' He looked towards the door. 'These people are amazing.' He glanced at her. 'You are beyond amazing.' Then he leaned down. Kissed her dry lips and tucked her in. 'Go back to sleep.'

When she woke in the morning Rayne was still there. His eyes were closed but for some reason she didn't think he was asleep. The drips had stopped feeding blood and had changed to clear fluid, so she guessed that was a good thing.

Connor was still sleeping. She reminded herself that babies could sleep up to ten or twelve hours after the first feed to get over the birth and she didn't need to feel guilty she hadn't fed him again. Remembered he'd probably make her pay for it later by feeding every time she wanted to put him back in his cot. Though she couldn't imagine wanting to put him back in his cot. It felt so long since she'd held him in her arms.

'Good morning.' Rayne's eyes were open. 'How do you feel?'

'I must look like a dishrag.'

'You look beautiful. A little pale and interesting as well.'

'At least I'm interesting.' She winced as she smiled too hard.

'I'll get Misty.' He left and came back with Misty, who was almost ready to hand her over to the morning staff.

So they repeated the whole Rayne lifting her, tablet taking, observation thing, and this time she didn't want to go back to sleep afterwards. She wanted to change out of her horrible gown and get into her nightie. Get up and shower, but she didn't think she'd be able to do it.

Could feel herself getting cross. 'Why don't you go back to the manse and have a sleep?'

Rayne lifted his brows and looked at her. Smiled. 'Later. When you have a wash, and get into your nightie, and have Connor's next feed. I don't know you well but I know you enough to see you want to be fresh, and hold your son, soon.'

He looked at her and shrugged. 'I want to help you, and help the midwife helping you, and I can be the muscle so you don't have to hurt yourself trying to do all those things.'

She looked at him. Flabbergasted. Was this guy for real? 'Aren't you tired?'

'No more than you. I'll sleep later.'

'I can't let you do that.'

Another enigmatic smile. 'You're not running this show, Princess Maeve. I am.'

Ooh. Bossy. She was too weak, and it was hard not to sort of like it. 'Then maybe later, if you're good, you can put me in the shower,' she said with a tired smile.

'I don't think you'll be up to a shower but we'll see.'

But she dug her heels in. 'I'm not being washed in bed like a baby.' They all looked at Rayne for help.

'Fine,' he said.

So they agreed on a compromise before Misty

went off. Once Maeve's pain tablets had kicked in and she wasn't too sore, they disconnected her IVs for the few minutes it would take, and Rayne lifted her to the edge of the bed then carried her to the shower chair and the hand-held shower nozzle, and gently hosed her all over, washed her back and her legs, until she began to feel human again. Amazing what some hot water and a change of position could do.

Misty made her bed up with fresh sheets and plumped up her pillows so that when Rayne had helped her dry and dress again she could sink back and relax.

'I'm walking back to the bed under my own steam.' She glared at him. He held up his hands.

'Your call. I'm happy to watch.'

So she eased herself into a standing position, and it wasn't too bad now that she'd loosened up. She tentatively took a few steps, knowing there was no way he would let her fall because his arms were right behind her. Not a bad feeling to have.

She straightened up more and she felt tender, but okay. She could do this. She looked up at Rayne to poke out her tongue, but then a wave of faintness caught up with her.

He must have seen the colour drain from her face because he said, 'No, you don't.' Before it could get too disastrous she found herself back in her bed, with Misty pulling up the sheets and saying, 'Someone needs to tell you about the blood you lost last night.'

When the world stopped turning she looked up to see Rayne frowning darkly at her. She thought vaguely that he was still too damn good looking even when he frowned. 'You're a stubborn woman.'

But Misty smiled at her as she tucked the sheets in. 'Stubborn women are the best kind because they never give in.'

Rayne rolled his eyes. 'Another mad midwife saying.'

Five minutes later Connor made a little snorting noise, and they both turned their heads to see, watched him shift in his cot, blink and then open his eyes.

'He's awake.'

Rayne saw the longing on Maeve's face and was so glad he'd stayed for this.

'Good morning, young man. Your mother has been through a lot while she waited for you to wake up.' He reached down and untucked the sheets and opened the bunny rug. A black tar train wreck lay inside. Was even glad he'd stayed for this. He'd cleaned up enough dirty nappies in his time to make short work of even the biggest mess and it seemed his son had quite a capacity. Go you, son.

Connor grumbled but didn't cry, as if confident of the handling he was receiving.

Rayne looked across at the bed and Maeve was holding her stomach to stop herself laughing, and they grinned at each other in mutual parental pride. Then he pinned up the new nappy efficiently and lifted Connor away from his bunny rug in his hospital clothes so Maeve could see his long legs and feet as he tucked him carefully in her arms.

Rayne watched her face soften and her mouth curve into such a smile, and the ball in his chest tightened and squeezed. This stuff had turned him into a wimp but he wouldn't have missed it for the world. He tucked a pillow under Maeve's arm so she didn't have to hold Connor's weight and watched as she loosened her neckline to lift out a breast.

Now, there was a sight he'd never tire of as Connor turned his head and poked out his tongue. Rayne put his hand under Connor's shoulders to help Maeve manoeuvre him closer until Connor opened his mouth, had a few practise attempts and then a big wide mouth and onto the breast. Just like that.

Maeve sighed and rested more comfortably back on the pillows, and Rayne sat back with wonder filling him until he thought he would burst.

My God.

How had this happened? Yesterday he had been lost, without purpose or future, a social misfit and almost-pariah, following his instinct towards a woman who so easily could have turned him away.

Now he had a family, Maeve and Connor and him—his family. And this morning he knew there would be battles of will, adjustments to make, discoveries and habits and ideas that might clash, but he could never doubt he had love for this incredible woman he had almost lost as soon as he'd found her, and that love would only grow bigger—probably daily. The future that was theirs stretched before them like a miracle. A Christmas miracle.

Rayne looked with wonder at the big country-style clock on the wall and watched the hand click over to six-thirty a.m. Exactly twenty-four hours since his car had rolled down the street and swerved towards the woman he'd been searching for as she'd walked towards him.

'Rayne?' Maeve's voice was softly concerned. 'You okay?'

He shook his head. The room was blurry. Stood up and stepped in close to the bed, leant down and slid his arm around the two of them and gently rested his cheek on Maeve's hair. He'd just discovered that she made him feel brand new. That he could do anything. And he most certainly was the only man for this job of looking after his family. 'I need to hug the most important two people in my life.'

She rested back into his arms with a contented sigh. 'Feel free any time.'

* * *

Over the next day there were a lot of firsts.

Connor's first bath, a joyous occasion where Maeve sat like a princess packed up in pillows and watched while Rayne deftly floated and massaged and swirled his son around like he'd been doing it for years.

'You're so good at that,' Maeve said approvingly. 'Still, I always tell the mums it's nice to shower with your baby. One of the parents undresses and hands baby in to go skin to skin with the person in the shower and the other— that will be you Rayne.' She grinned up at him. 'You lost. You just get to take him back and dry and dress him while I have the fun part.'

Rayne grinned. 'Poor me. I have to watch the naked lady with the awesome breasts in the shower with my baby.' Maeve held her tummy and tried not to laugh.

Then came the visitors with hugs and kisses of relief.

Also along came things for Connor. His first knitted set of bonnet, booties, cardigan and shawl all lovingly created by his step-great-grandmother, Louisa, who also brought food just in case the hospital ran out.

His first pair of tiny jeans and black T-shirt to match his dad's, from Uncle Simon and Tara.

Goodness knew where he'd got it from, because he'd barely left her side, but Rayne produced a bright yellow rubber duck for Connor's bath because his mother loved ducks.

Tiny booties shaped like soccer boots with knitted bumps for spikes from Mia and the girls at morning teatime and a welcome-baby card that had a three-dimensional baby actually swinging in a seat from a tree that the girls had fallen in love with.

But the excitement all took its toll.

'You look exhausted. Enough. I'll go back to the manse and you sleep.' Rayne stood up.

It was lunchtime, and Maeve was ready for a sleep.

Rayne kissed her. 'I'll come back any time you need me. If you want to get out of bed or Connor is unsettled and you want someone to nurse him, I'm the man. Ring me.' He looked at her. 'Promise.'

'Bossy.'

'Please.'

'Okay.' Not a bad back-up plan. She watched him go with a prickle of weak tears in her eyes and sighed into the bed.

'He did well,' Tara said, as she closed the blinds of the room.

'He did amazingly.'

'You did amazingly. But I agree with you and with him. It's time for sleep.' She checked Connor was fast asleep after his feed and quietly backed out.

As the door shut Maeve relaxed back into the bed and glanced at her downy-cheeked son. It had happened. She couldn't tell if he looked like either of them because now he looked like her darling baby Connor.

The whole labour and birth were over. And the next stage was just beginning.

The beginning of shared parenthood with a man she knew she loved. She didn't know if Rayne felt the same, but she was too tired and tender to worry about that now. That he was here was enough.

Rayne's solid support had been a thousand times stronger than she'd dared to hope for, his pre-birth nerves were a precious memory to keep and maybe occasionally tease him about, and she could see that Rayne would take his responsibilities to Connor and to her very seriously.

Lying in Rayne's arms yesterday seemed so far away in time with what had happened since then but as she drifted off to sleep she knew there was so much they could build on. She just needed to be patient, she thought with sleepy smile on her face, and trust in Rayne.

CHAPTER ELEVEN

FOUR DAYS LATER Maeve went home with Connor and Rayne—her family. Home being to the manse and the fabulous cooking of Louisa, who had decided the new mother needed feeding up.

Rayne, being fed three meals a day at least, was chopping wood at an alarming rate to try and keep his weight down from Louisa's cooking.

Simon went back to Sydney for work and planned to return each alternate weekend, and Tara was going to fly down to Sydney on the other weekends until their wedding in four weeks' time.

Selfishly, Maeve was glad that Tara had stayed

with them, instead of following Simon to Sydney, and with Rayne booked to do the occasional shift over in the hospital on call, she had ample back-up help with Tara and, of course, Louisa, who was in seventh heaven with a baby in the house.

They'd shifted Connor into Rayne's room with the connecting door open and Rayne bounced out of their bed to change and bring Connor to her through the night.

Life took on a rosy glow of contentment as she and Rayne and Connor grew to be a family. The joy of waking in the morning in Rayne's tender arms, the wonder on his face when he looked at her with Connor, the gradual healing of her body, the steady increase of confidence in breastfeeding, managing Connor's moods and signs of tiredness, and the ability to hand him to his father's outstretched hands all gelled. Life was wonderful.

Her brother's wedding approached and their

mother was coming. It was four weeks after the birth of Connor and Maeve was suddenly nervous.

Rayne decided Maeve had been twitchy all morning. Her mother was due to arrive along with Maeve's three older sisters. He'd seen her change her clothes four times and Connor's jumpsuit twice before the expected event.

On arrival her mother kissed Maeve's cheek and an awkward few moments had passed right at the beginning when she looked Rayne over with a sigh and then stepped forward and shook his hand.

'Hello, Rayne. Maeve said you were very good when Connor was born.'

So this was what Maeve would look like when she was older. Stunning, sophisticated and polished, though Desiree was blonde, perhaps not naturally because she had dark eyebrows, but a very successful-looking blonde.

He glanced at Maeve and the woman holding his son had it all over her mum for warmth. 'It was Maeve who was amazing.'

A cool smile. 'I'm glad she's happy.'

'So am I.' Which left what either of them really meant open to interpretation.

Maeve broke into the conversation. 'You remember my sisters, Ellen, Claire and Stephanie.'

'Ladies.' He smiled at the three women, who were cooing at Connor.

Maeve hung onto his hand and Connor was unusually unsettled, probably receptive to the vibes his mother was giving off.

Luckily Desiree was swept up into the final wedding preparations and they all managed to ease back on the tension for the rest of the afternoon.

The next day Simon and Tara's wedding was held in the little local church and most of the town had come to celebrate with them.

It was a simple and incredibly romantic celebration. The church ladies had excelled themselves with floral decorations. Tara looked like the fairy on top of the cake, thanks to the absolute delight Mia, Simon's stepmother, had taken in spoiling her, and beside him, Simon nearly cried in the church when she entered.

A big lump had come to Rayne's throat when he thought about his friend finding such happiness and he couldn't help his glance past the bride and groom to the chief bridesmaid, his Maeve, who looked incredible in the simple blue gown Tara had chosen for her attendants.

Except for the divine cleavage, nobody would suspect Maeve had recently given birth, because she'd returned to her pre-pregnancy size almost immediately.

As Rayne listened to the words of the priest the certainty inside him grew that he could answer yes to all of it.

By the time Simon and Tara were married all

he wanted to do was hold Maeve in his arms and tell her he loved her.

But he would have to wait.

The reception was a huge outdoor picnic, all the speeches a success, and the ecstatically happy couple finally left for their honeymoon in Hawaii and would then fly on to Boston, where Maeve's father waited to meet his stepson's new wife.

Back at the manse after the wedding Rayne needed a beer and a bloke to drink with, because the only sane woman was Louisa, who kept feeding him.

Maeve still hadn't settled, though she seemed to stress more than anything about Connor being even a little upset, which was strange when before she'd sailed along blithely and just enjoyed him. The help from her mother wasn't doing its job.

Rayne decided he would survive until Maeve's

mother left. He'd lived with worse people and his lips twitched. Could just imagine Maeve's mother's downturned mouth if she knew he was comparing her to a cellmate.

'There you are, Rayne.' The object of his thoughts appeared and he plastered a smile on his face.

'Connor is crying and Maeve asked for you. Though I can't see what you can do that I can't.'

'Thank you.' Excellent reason to escape. 'The wedding was great but I think everyone is tired now. I'd better go and see.'

When he gently opened the door to their room he found Maeve with tears trickling down her face as Connor screamed and kicked and fought the breast.

'Hey, Connor, what are you doing to your poor mum?'

Maeve looked up tragically and he crossed the room to sit beside her on the bed. He dropped a kiss on her head. 'He won't feed. And Mum keeps telling me to put him on the bottle.'

'Bless her,' Rayne said, tongue-in-cheek and Maeve's eyes flew to his, ready to hotly dispute that, until she saw his smile.

Her own smile, while still watery, gradually appeared. 'She makes me crazy.'

'Really? I hadn't noticed.' He leaned forward, kissed her, remembered again how each day he felt more blessed, and took the unsettled Connor from her. Tucked him over his shoulder and patted his bottom. 'It's been a big day. And you've been busy making sure Tara had a fabulous time so you've run yourself into the ground. Why don't I take Connor for a drive and you can have a rest before tea?'

'No, thanks.'

Maeve looked even sadder and he frowned. 'What?'

'Can't I come with you both?'

He grinned. 'You mean escape? And leave your mother here without us?'

Maeve looked guilty at the disloyal idea. 'She means well.'

'I know. Maybe we could get Louisa to look after her. Your mum's probably tired too. It's a long flight and she only got here yesterday.' He had a vision. One that he'd been building up to for days now but had wanted to leave until after the wedding. 'I'd really like to take Connor to the duck pond. Would you like to come with us for an hour until sunset?'

Maeve nodded, looked brighter already, so he left her to get ready, and sought out Louisa first, begged a favour he promised to repay, then found Maeve's mother.

Gently does it, he warned himself. 'What do you think if I take Connor for a little drive. Just to get him asleep in the car?'

A judicious nod from the dragon. 'That's an excellent idea.'

Now for the smooth part. 'Maeve wants to come but she feels bad about leaving you on your own.' Desiree opened her mouth but before she could invite herself he said, 'But I see Louisa had just made you a lovely afternoon tea and is dying to have a good chat with you. What would you like to do?' Opened his eyes wide.

Desiree slid gracefully into the trap and relief expanded in his gut. 'Oh. Poor Louisa. It would be rude not to stay for that. Of course.' She looked pleased. 'How thoughtful. She really is a lovely woman.'

'One of my favourite people.' And wasn't that true. Then he escaped to his family and bundled them into the car.

Ten minutes later Maeve sat on the bench in front of the lake, holding Connor in the crook of her arm. Their son had decided he preferred to feed alfresco and was very happily feeding.

Every now and then Maeve would throw bread-crumbs to the ducks with her free hand.

Rayne stood behind her, gently rubbing her shoulders. They both had smiles on their faces.

Maeve said, 'I don't think I could bear to lose a man who rubs my shoulders like you do.'

Rayne felt the happiness expand inside him. 'Does this mean you want me to stay?'

She twisted her neck to look at him and pre-tended to consider it judiciously. 'Yes, I think so.'

Rayne had waited for just this opening and unfortunately in the euphoria of successful strategies he rushed it. 'Only if you'll marry me.' The words were out before he could stop them and he cursed his inability to be smooth and romantic when she deserved it all. He'd done everything the wrong way around here.

She opened her mouth to reply and quickly he moved around to face her and held up his finger. 'Wait.'

'So bossy,' she murmured, and he smiled as he went down on one knee beside her—right there in front of the ducks.

'Please. Wait for me to do it properly.' He took her free hand in his, brushed the crumbs off it and kissed her fingers. Maeve leant back against the bench and Connor ignored them both as he continued with his afternoon tea.

Rayne drew a deep breath and let it go. Let everything go, let the past, the mistakes and the pain and uncertainty all go so they could start fresh and new and perfect. Because the three of them deserved it. 'My darling, gorgeous, sexy…' he paused, smiled at her '…impossible Maeve—'

Before he could finish she'd interrupted. 'Impossible?'

'Shh.' He frowned at her and she closed her mouth. 'Darling Maeve—' and he couldn't keep the smile off his face '—will you do me the honour, please, of becoming my wife and share with me the rest of my life?'

Her face glowed at him, a trace of pink dusting the high cheekbones that were still far too pale. 'Now, that, as a proposal of marriage, was worth waiting for.'

'An answer would be good. Come on.'

She teased him. 'My darling, strong, sexy as all get out Rayne.' Leaned forward and kissed him while he knelt before her. Connor still ignored them both. 'Yes. Please. Pretty please. I would love to be your wife and share your life.'

His relief expanded and he squeezed her hand. 'You won't regret it.'

Her face softened. 'I know I won't. But my mother wants a big wedding.'

He smiled. He could do that. It was a small price to pay for the world he now had. 'I thought she might. As long as Connor is pageboy and you are my bride, I will agree to anything.'

He stood up and hugged her gently again and smiled into her hair. 'It's not going to be dull.'

A month later Maeve woke on the morning of her wedding in her parents' house huge in Boston. Down the hall Tara was sleeping without her new husband because Simon had gone to support Rayne on the night before his wedding. She wished she'd been able to stay with Rayne but they would never have got that past her mother.

Connor stirred beside her and she sat up with a warm feeling of relief in her stomach and reached for him. Rayne would be missing Connor and her as much as they missed him.

How could life change so dramatically in just two months? The answer was simple. Rayne loved her. Which was lucky because her mother had put them all through hoops as she married the first of her daughters off in the grand fashion.

There had been family dinners at exclusive restaurants, wedding breakfasts under the marquee in the back garden, and bridal teas with all the local ladies, as well as bridal showers and multiple rehearsals and today, finally, the wedding of the year.

Maeve had always wanted a big wedding, the chance to be the big star, but funnily enough now that it was here she knew she would have been happy with a two-line agreement in front of a celebrant as long as she was married to Rayne.

Her mother wouldn't have been happy, though, and it was good to see Desiree finally pleased with her. But today she would marry Rayne, they would pack up and leave on their honeymoon then head back to Lyrebird Lake, and Maeve couldn't wait.

Her husband-to-be had been amazing. Patient. Comforting when she'd become stressed, loving when she'd least expected it but had secretly needed that reassurance, and always so brilliantly patient and capable with Connor—and her mother.

When she thought about it, Rayne had learnt to be patient with mothers very early in his life and he was showing his skills now.

Her over-achieving sisters were here and she realised she'd finally grown out of worrying that about a hundred relatives were scattered in nearby hotels. She and Rayne and Connor were united in the birth of their family and their future and she couldn't wait.

Eight hours later Rayne stood beside Simon, this time as the groom and Simon the best man, and Rayne's hands were just slightly shaking.

In Boston, their bigger than *Ben Hur* wedding that Maeve's mother had organised had seemed to never get any closer.

But finally, today, it would happen. Their family would officially be joined forever. Maeve was putting so much trust in him he felt humbled, and before God, and before the ceremony even started, he silently vowed he would never let her down.

The music started, the congregation stood, and then she was there. A heartbeat, a shaft of divine light, and she appeared. Standing at the end of that very long, very floral-bouqueted aisle, with her father beside her and a huge church full of people to witness them being bound together.

Maeve's next older sister, the first bridesmaid, was almost up to them, coming closer with stately precision, Connor in her arms in his tiny suit, because that was the only thing Rayne had insisted on.

Then the second sister, and then the third, and then…Maeve. Sweeping down the aisle towards him, way too fast. To hell with the slow walk, he didn't bother to look for her mother's frown at the break in protocol, just grinned at her and held out his hand. He loved this woman so much.

The mass began and he missed most of it as he stared at the vision beside him. Remembered the last two months, the joy he'd found, the deep well of love he hadn't realised he'd had to give.

'Do you take this woman…?'

Hell, yes! He remembered to let the reverend finish. More waiting until finally he could say, 'I will.'

'Do you, Maeve, take this man…?'

The words drifted as he stared again into her eyes. Those eloquent eyes that said he was her hero, always would be, that she believed in him so much and loved him. What more could a man want?

Then she said, 'I will.' That was what he wanted!

'With the power vested in me and before this congregation I now declare you man and wife…' And it was done. Rayne lifted the veil, stared into her tear-filled eyes and kissed his wife with all the love in his heart in the salute.

Maeve clutched her husband's hand and couldn't help the huge smile on her face. The cameras were flashing, she was moving and signing and smiling, and all the time Rayne was beside her. Protecting her, loving her, and finally reaching out to take Connor from her sister so that he carried their son and it was time for the three of them to walk back up the aisle as a family.

Maeve met Rayne's eyes, saw the love and knew this was the start of an incredible life with the man she had always loved. She couldn't wait.

* * * * *

MILLS & BOON®
Large Print Medical

July

HOW TO FIND A MAN IN FIVE DATES	Tina Beckett
BREAKING HER NO-DATING RULE	Amalie Berlin
IT HAPPENED ONE NIGHT SHIFT	Amy Andrews
TAMED BY HER ARMY DOC'S TOUCH	Lucy Ryder
A CHILD TO BIND THEM	Lucy Clark
THE BABY THAT CHANGED HER LIFE	Louisa Heaton

August

A DATE WITH HER VALENTINE DOC	Melanie Milburne
IT HAPPENED IN PARIS...	Robin Gianna
THE SHEIKH DOCTOR'S BRIDE	Meredith Webber
TEMPTATION IN PARADISE	Joanna Neil
A BABY TO HEAL THEIR HEARTS	Kate Hardy
THE SURGEON'S BABY SECRET	Amber McKenzie

September

BABY TWINS TO BIND THEM	Carol Marinelli
THE FIREFIGHTER TO HEAL HER HEART	Annie O'Neil
TORTURED BY HER TOUCH	Dianne Drake
IT HAPPENED IN VEGAS	Amy Ruttan
THE FAMILY SHE NEEDS	Sue MacKay
A FATHER FOR POPPY	Abigail Gordon

MILLS & BOON®
Large Print Medical

October

JUST ONE NIGHT?	Carol Marinelli
MEANT-TO-BE FAMILY	Marion Lennox
THE SOLDIER SHE COULD NEVER FORGET	Tina Beckett
THE DOCTOR'S REDEMPTION	Susan Carlisle
WANTED: PARENTS FOR A BABY!	Laura Iding
HIS PERFECT BRIDE?	Louisa Heaton

November

ALWAYS THE MIDWIFE	Alison Roberts
MIDWIFE'S BABY BUMP	Susanne Hampton
A KISS TO MELT HER HEART	Emily Forbes
TEMPTED BY HER ITALIAN SURGEON	Louisa George
DARING TO DATE HER EX	Annie Claydon
THE ONE MAN TO HEAL HER	Meredith Webber

December

MIDWIFE...TO MUM!	Sue MacKay
HIS BEST FRIEND'S BABY	Susan Carlisle
ITALIAN SURGEON TO THE STARS	Melanie Milburne
HER GREEK DOCTOR'S PROPOSAL	Robin Gianna
NEW YORK DOC TO BLUSHING BRIDE	Janice Lynn
STILL MARRIED TO HER EX!	Lucy Clark

0615 LP 2P P2 N